A Candlelight Ecstasy Romance™

LIKE A BOLT OUT OF THE BLUE THE KNOWLEDGE HIT HER. . . .

She loved him. The realization sent tingles of sudden awareness along her nerve endings. She loved him!

And now she knew why she had felt a fleeting shock of recognition when they had first met. She *had* known him. He was every hero she had ever devised for her books. He was the faceless man in the dreams that had haunted her for years.

He was her destiny.

CANDLELIGHT ECSTASY ROMANCES™

MASK OF PASSION

Kay Hooper

A CANDLELIGHT ECSTASY ROMANCE™

Published by
Dell Publishing Co., Inc.
1 Dag Hammarskjold Plaza
New York, New York 10017

Dell ® TM 681510, Dell Publishing Co., Inc.

Candlelight Ecstasy Romance™ is a trademark of
Dell Publishing Co., Inc., New York, New York.

ISBN: 0–440–15406–5

Printed in the United States of America
First printing—August 1982

Dear Reader:

In response to your continued enthusiasm for Candlelight Ecstasy Romances™, we are increasing the number of new titles from four to six per month.

We are delighted to present sensuous novels set in America, depicting modern American men and women as they confront the provocative problems of modern relationships.

Throughout the history of the Candlelight line, Dell has tried to maintain a high standard of excellence, to give you the finest in reading enjoyment. That is now and will remain our most ardent ambition.

Anne Gisonny
Editor
Candlelight Romances

*To my parents, for their love and support . . .
and that Christmas typewriter so long ago.*

CHAPTER ONE

Danica Morgan's vivid green eyes were blank with surprise as she stared at the middle-aged man sprawled comfortably in his chair behind a massive oak desk. "You have a warped sense of humor, Jason," she said slowly, her voice a little uncertain.

Jason Carrington's gray eyes held a glint of unholy amusement. "You heard what I said. Bay Spencer wants you in his new film."

She leaned forward suddenly. "You're serious, aren't you. You're really serious."

"Never more so." He laughed suddenly. "Spencer's trying to track you down now, so I thought I'd better warn you. In case you want to leave the country or something."

Danica, looking cool and elegant in a leaf-green silk dress, did not seem amused by his teasing. "For heaven's sake, Jason, doesn't the man know I'm not an actress?"

"Of course, he knows," Jason snorted. "Bill Evans over at World Pictures told me that Spencer walked into his office a couple of weeks ago, slapped a magazine down on his desk, and told him that he'd found a girl to play the

11

title role in his film. He pointed at the cover and—behold! —Danica Morgan."

She latched on to the most important part of this speech. "Title role?" The amusement in his eyes deepened and put Danica further on her guard. "Just what *is* Spencer's new film?"

Jason assumed a childlike innocence. "Why, Dany, I'm surprised at you! The film isn't even in production yet, and already there's been a great deal of publicity about it— don't tell me you haven't heard it!"

Dany felt a feeling of foreboding creep over her. "Jason, what film is Spencer going to produce?"

Jason dropped his bomb with all the air of one who knows exactly how it will be received. "The film, my dear Dany, is *Serena;* and Spencer wants you for the title role." He was honestly delighted with the expression of horror on her lovely face. A generation older than her, he had known her since she was a child, but it had been only since the death of her parents, five years before, that they had become close.

And since that time, he had watched her assume a succession of masks, wearing each one like a shield to protect herself from the probing of others. After nearly five years she had developed that technique to a fine art, and it was rare that her veneer of sophistication cracked to reveal her true feelings.

In spite of the fact that Danica Morgan was one of the highest paid models in the country, and in spite of the fact that her innocently beautiful face had adorned the covers of dozens of magazines during the past few years, she had managed to keep her private life very much a mystery. She attended few of the high-class parties she was invited to, never gave interviews, and avoided the limelight with an almost fanatical intensity.

Jason Carrington, the guiding spirit behind Castle Publishing Company, eyed his favorite author with humor. "I found it very amusing," he explained kindly, "that Spencer chose the *creator* of Serena to play the *part* of Serena."

Dany closed her mouth with a snap and glared at him. For the first time since entering the office, the temper advertised by her copper-gold hair was letting itself be seen. "There isn't anything amusing about it, Jason! From what I've heard about Spencer, this will be a major film. Do you seriously expect me to believe that he wants to cast an unknown in the title role?"

Jason sobered abruptly. "You're hardly that, Dany. Your face has been on the cover of every major magazine lately, and I can't turn on the television without seeing those perfume commercials you've been doing. No, my dear, you have one of the most visible faces in the world."

"Which doesn't alter the fact that I'm not an actress! At the end of the year my contract with the agency runs out, and after that I don't plan to pose for anything except vacation pictures!"

Keen gray eyes surveyed her thoughtfully. "You've never enjoyed being in the public eye, have you, Dany?"

Dany sat back and made a visible effort to calm down. "No," she said in a calmer voice. "I haven't. I only became a model because I thought it would be a good way to earn a living while I was writing my first book. You suggested it, if you'll remember! I never would have done it if I had known that things would skyrocket the way they did."

Jason chuckled softly. "Skyrocket—that's certainly an apt way of putting it. That first year, you became successful in two different professions: modeling and writing novels."

Her delicately curved lips twisted slightly. "And you seriously expect me to tackle a third career?" Her brows drew together in a faint frown. "When does Spencer plan to begin filming?"

"In August."

"And today is the first of May." The frown disappeared. "There's no problem, then. I had planned to fly out to Portland tomorrow and drive to the coast. I'll spend the summer at home. The agency will inform Spencer that I don't want the part, and he'll just have to find someone else to take the role."

Jason grinned slightly. "You're a coward, Dany. Why don't you just meet Spencer and refuse the part?"

Her smile was a little rueful. "Because I don't want to be forced to explain my reasons to him. The only ones who know that Aurora Sanders, author of *A Time for Serena,* is actually myself, are you and I—and that's the way I want it to remain."

"You don't have to tell him that, you know. Just say that you aren't interested in becoming an actress."

Dany rose to move restlessly about the spacious room, her slender body alive with a fluid grace. "From the little I've heard of Bay Spencer, he doesn't seem like the type of man who takes no for an answer."

"You're right about that." Jason nodded slowly. "He has a reputation for getting exactly what he wants." He watched her aimless wandering for a moment before asking curiously, "What did you think of the screenplay?"

She moved to stare out the window at the traffic on Park Avenue, far below. Parrying his question with one of her own, she said, "I meant to ask you who adapted the novel. I was never told which writer the studio settled on."

He waited until she turned to face him before replying, "Bay Spencer."

Her expression was resigned rather than surprised. "I had a feeling somehow that you were going to say that."

Amusement lightened his craggy features as Jason shrugged. "I can't help it if the man's talented, Dany. He

14

adapted the screenplay from your novel, he's doing the casting, and he'll produce *and* direct the film."

She had turned back to the window. "If you ask me, Mr. Bay Spencer has a problem."

Jason lifted a questioning eyebrow. "Oh? And what would that be?"

"A lack of confidence." Over her shoulder she smiled at him with sweet sarcasm.

He smiled, but there was a faint look of censure in his eyes, causing her to stir impatiently. "Oh, I know I'm not being reasonable, Jason, but I can't stand men who think they know everything."

"You're not being very fair to Spencer, Dany. For all you know, he may have the Midas touch where films are concerned. He certainly did well with the one he produced last year."

"And the year before that." Seeing the sudden spark of interest in Jason's eyes, Dany went on hurriedly. "He can't know very much about casting, or he wouldn't have chosen me for the part of Serena."

Quietly Jason responded, "I think he knows a great deal about casting—at least in this case. You *are* Serena."

She stared at him. "Jason, Serena is simply a character that I dreamed up. I wanted to write a novel about a model, and Serena was the result. She's no more like me than any of my other characters are."

He laced his fingers over his thickening waist and smiled slightly. "Are you sure about that, Dany?"

When she turned merely to stare once again out the window, Jason began to speak softly. "Serena is you. She is an incredibly lovely young woman who never realized how beautiful she was until she became almost an overnight success in the modeling profession. Intelligent, sensitive, and vulnerable, she learned to hide how easily she could be hurt. She hated the cold cynicism of the business

15

she was in and hated the fact that men seemed to take her at face value. She fought the sponsors and advertisers who tried to buy their way into her bed, because her innocent, alluring beauty hid a strong moral sense that was as rare as it was out of step with the times."

There was a long silence, and then he added gently, "*You* are Serena."

She took a deep breath and, without turning, said almost inaudibly, "You should hang out a shingle. You'd make a pretty fair psychologist."

"I've spent half my life dealing with temperamental writers, Dany. I've learned to see beneath the surface."

Finally admitting something that she had denied even to herself, Dany said quietly, "All right. There *is* more of me in Serena than in any of my other characters. That being the case, can you imagine what would happen if I took the role that Spencer's offering? Some enterprising reporter would be bound to spot the similarities between Danica Morgan and Serena, and then to find a connection to Aurora Sanders." She shook her head. "I won't chance that."

He sighed regretfully. "I suppose you're right. You would have been a smash though, Dany. Spencer will never find anyone as right for the part as you are." He chuckled suddenly. "Lord, but he'll be in a temper! When he isn't able to contact you through the agency, he'll probably come here looking for you. It's common knowledge that you and I have been friends for years."

She turned from the window with a rueful smile. "Don't you mean it's common knowledge that the two of us are lovers? At least that's what I heard."

He grinned. "I wondered if you'd heard that. I must say that it's very flattering for a man of my age to be linked with you."

"And what does Christine think of the rumors?"

Secure in a supremely happy marriage, Jason was still amused. "Oh, Christine knows that she's all the woman I can handle. Besides, we both think of you as another daughter—you know that."

Since the Carringtons *were* like a second set of parents to her, Dany readily believed him. When her mother and father had been killed in a car crash five years before, she had been very grateful for the Carringtons' support. They never interfered in her personal life, any more than they interfered in the life of their daughter, Jeannie, who lived in Europe.

Dany shot a thoughtful look at Jason and decided that she wouldn't tell him how the rumors about their supposed affair had helped her. She had denied it in the beginning, but that had only seemed to make people believe it all the more, so she had decided to ignore it. After a time, she had been relieved to see that men weren't quite so determined in their pursuit of her when they believed that she was the mistress of a powerful, wealthy man. It was certainly not the method she would have chosen to ward off her admirers, but she had been desperate enough at that point to accept it gratefully.

She was aware that such a thing could seriously disrupt her personal life—should the right man come along. But she had been granted very little time during the past few years for a personal life of any kind, and she was firm in the belief that if a man fell in love with her—for herself— he would surely see that she was not the type of woman that rumor had painted her to be.

Dany was not a vain young woman, in spite of the attention and admiration she had received over the years. She had never considered herself to be beautiful, and the realization that men seemed to find her enormously seductive had both baffled and alarmed her. The first man who had offered her bed and board—without the benefit of wedding ring—had been given a scathing reply, but she had been shocked to discover that he was only the first of many.

Shocked dismay had hardened into grim resignation since that time, and she had come to consider her unusual beauty as a curse rather than a blessing. If she had not been under contract with the agency, she would have vanished from sight as soon as she discovered that she could earn her living writing, but she felt a strong sense of obligation to honor her commitments. So she had continued to accept assignments and grew more and more reclusive in her private life.

Independently minded, Dany had not shed tears on her pillow at night because of the lack of male companionship in her life, but she had not quite abandoned the rosy dreams she had had since childhood. They came back to haunt her occasionally when she saw two lovers strolling arm in arm, or a young mother with a baby on her hip. She would feel a twinge of loneliness—an odd, empty ache inside—but she always pushed the feeling away. She was too intelligent to believe that she would find the happiness she sought in the arms of a man who wanted only to possess her.

She had never yet allowed any man to get close enough to see beneath the mask she wore; men were attracted to the image that she presented to the world. And that was not Danica Morgan.

At twenty-five Dany had buried her romantic dreams of love and marriage, pulling them from the depths of her being only when she sat before the typewriter, creating for her characters the happy endings she craved for herself.

Suddenly aware that she had been silent for some time, Dany met Jason's probing gaze with a faint smile. In the same curious voice that he had used before, he said, "You

18

never did tell me what you thought of Spencer's screen-play."

She moved back to the chair in front of the desk and sank down with her peculiar flowing grace. "To tell you the truth it staggered me," she confessed wryly. "Serena's character was captured with amazing perception. I wouldn't have thought Spencer capable of it."

Slowly Jason said, "That's the second time I've gotten the impression that you know more about Spencer than I thought. Have you met him?"

"No. But I've heard of him from other models, and from some of the television people." Her voice was without expression, but her vivid emerald eyes glittered with dislike as she remembered some of the things she had heard. Cold, arrogant, inconsiderate, insensitive, sarcastic, bad-tempered, demanding—all were adjectives she had heard in connection with Spencer. She wasn't foolish enough to believe everything, of course, but even allowing for exaggeration, he seemed to be the sort of autocratic personality that she most disliked.

Conversely he also seemed the sort of man who managed to induce women to collapse at his feet. Dany had wondered more than once how he was able to make women fall in love with him when he appeared to treat them with almost brutal indifference. She knew personally of at least three models who had had crying fits after having been rather crudely abandoned by him. To hear them tell it, the man was a monster of cruelty—and they would have happily given their right arms to be back in his good graces. It appeared that Spencer could be both loved and hated at the same time—at least by women.

In all fairness, of course, Dany had to admit that the stories she had heard had all been decidedly one-sided. But her experiences with men had not been the kind to engender any emotion but contempt for men like Spencer.

She had never set eyes on him, but she disliked him intensely, and knowing that her dislike was unreasonable did nothing to lessen it.

The sound of Jason loudly clearing his throat brought Dany abruptly back to the present, and she looked up to see a gleam of amusement in his gray eyes.

"You looked as though you wanted to murder someone, Dany. I'd appreciate it if you wouldn't do that—I just had the carpet cleaned."

She smiled slightly. "Sorry, Jason. I was thinking."

"About Spencer? You know, Dany, for someone who has never met the man, you certainly seem to hate him."

She had the grace to look a little self-conscious. "Let's just say that I'm not very attracted to that type of man."

Jason didn't look convinced but allowed the matter to drop. "Are you going to spend the night at the apartment?"

Dany nodded. The apartment belonged to Jason—another thing that had lent weight to the rumors that she was his mistress—but he only kept it so that his out-of-town business associates wouldn't be forced to say at hotels. Since Dany was generally in New York only for brief periods, Jason insisted that she stay there rather than waste money on an apartment of her own, which would remain empty for most of the year.

She stood and reached for her purse. "If Spencer should get in touch with you, Jason, just tell him that I've gone on vacation and you haven't the faintest idea where I can be reached."

"He won't believe me," Jason responded wryly.

She smiled. "Probably not, but it doesn't matter. By the time he thinks to check your apartment, I should be long gone."

"Anyone would think you were afraid of the man," he commented as he walked her to the door.

Dany laughed, and was amused when he bent to kiss her cheek as he opened the door. Perfectly aware—from the glint of mischief in his eyes—that he had made the gesture because his flustered secretary was standing on the other side of the door with one hand raised to knock, she cast him a shaming look.

He laughed in response, his gray eyes twinkling as he turned his gaze to the red-faced girl. "What is it, Ann?"

"I'm sorry, sir. But there's a Mr. Spencer on the phone, and he won't be put off!" The secretary seemed considerably aggrieved, from which Dany gathered that Spencer had been employing his normal roughshod tactics.

"Speak of the Devil," she murmured, and brushed past the girl to head for the outer door. "See you later, Jason."

"Dinner tonight," he called after her, and waited for her smiling nod before going back inside his office to take care of the insistent Mr. Spencer.

Knowing ruefully that the entire outer office staff believed that she had just agreed to an assignation with Jason, Dany decided that it was a good thing she didn't mind all the rumors; another juicy tidbit had just been added to the pot. She made a mental note to call Christine and tell her that her "other daughter" was back in town, and had been invited to dinner, because Jason would be certain to forget to call his wife.

She rode down to the ground floor in the elevator and stepped out of the building into the weak May sunshine, feeling a sense of freedom as she realized that tomorrow's plane would be the last she would have to catch for a while. She had spent the past six weeks flying all over Europe for a fashion layout, and she was utterly weary of napping on planes and eating on the run. She was looking forward to relaxing on the deck of her beach house and listening to a soothing, wonderfully undemanding ocean.

With a faint sigh Dany started down the street, glad

that Jason's apartment was located only a block away. A glance at her watch showed that she would have time for a long, leisurely bath and a short nap before Jason came to pick her up—which he always did, in spite of her protests.

A few minutes later she was nodding to the doorman and responding to his polite "Good afternoon, Miss Morgan."

"Good afternoon, Robert." A sudden thought made her pause in the doorway. "Robert . . . has there been a gentleman here in the last week or so asking for me?"

The middle-aged doorman's face was impassive. "Yes, Miss Morgan. The same gentleman came several times during the past few days. He came again this afternoon, and was told that you were not expected in the near future."

Amusement glimmered in her eyes as Dany smiled slightly. It was quite possible that she was suffering from jet lag, but she could distinctly remember speaking to Robert when she had dropped her bags off at the apartment just before lunchtime. The doorman had obviously assumed that Spencer had been angling for an introduction, and had treated him just the way he had treated every other man who had tried to locate Dany during the past months. Jason's orders, she knew.

I'll bet Mr. Hotshot Producer didn't like that one bit! she thought in amusement. Stepping past the patient doorman, Dany said quietly, "Thank you, Robert."

"Of course, Miss Morgan." He bowed slightly and let the door swing gently closed, leaving her alone in the quiet lobby.

She rode the elevator up to the penthouse and used her key to let herself into the apartment. She closed the door behind her and smiled at the dignified elderly man moving into the entranceway to greet her. "Good afternoon, Jenkins."

"Good afternoon, Miss Morgan." Jenkins's voice was as stiffly British as she remembered, and she wondered, as she always did, how he had managed to retain his accent after more than twenty years in the States.

"I'll be dining with the Carringtons tonight, Jenkins, and catching the nine o'clock flight to Portland in the morning."

He nodded. "Very well, miss."

Dany headed for her bedroom, wondering curiously what the old gentleman thought of her. Since he had been Jason's houseman for twenty years, he probably thought of her as another daughter of the family. If he had heard the rumors regarding her relationship with his employer, he certainly didn't let on that he had.

Ignoring the familiar luxury of the sunken living room done in shades of gold and rust, Dany moved down the long hall to her royal blue and white bedroom. She kicked her high-heeled shoes off the moment she entered the room, and then padded barefoot across the plush carpet to the adjoining bath.

It, too, was blue and white, the major feature being the sunken tub in the middle of the spacious room. Dany bent to turn the faucets on full force, and then paused just long enough to sprinkle bubble bath in the water before going back into the bedroom.

Her cases stood at the foot of the king-size bed, still packed, since she had sent word to Jenkins to leave them that way. She chose one and placed it on the bed, opening it to reveal the jumble of clothing she had packed hastily in order to catch that last flight out of London.

With a slight grimace Dany pawed through the tangle until she found her robe, then went to close the hall door before swiftly getting undressed. She picked up the robe

23

and carried it into the bathroom, dropping it onto a stool and then sinking gratefully into the steaming hot water.

While she allowed her body to relax in the scented water, Dany wondered rather grimly if she could bear to continue modeling for the remainder of the year. Whoever made the statement that models had it easy had never talked to one. The hours were long and the pace was grueling; the effort of being forced to hold a smile or a pose for what seemed like forever was as exhausting as it was tedious.

Dany glanced around at the opulent luxury of the bathroom and sighed softly. This wasn't what she wanted either. She wasn't comfortable in these surroundings. That was probably why she never remained here long, but always beat a hasty retreat to her beach house on the coast of Oregon—where she didn't feel guilty if she wanted to dress in cutoff jeans, or eat a peanut butter sandwich in the den.

She sighed again. It was not hard to pretend to feel at ease with such luxury—necessary, in fact. Few people would believe that she could easily turn away from a life filled with "the beautiful people" and elegant surroundings. But she could.

She would gladly have traded every bit of her fame as a model for the chance to putter happily around the beach and write to her heart's content.

The intercom buzzed just then, and Dany glared irritably at yet another symbol of luxury before stretching out an arm to press the button. "What is it, Jenkins?"

"I beg your pardon, miss, but it's Mr. Hamilton on the telephone. He insists on speaking to you."

Having a very good idea what the owner of her modeling agency wanted to talk to her about, Dany let out a resigned sigh. "Tell him to hang on, Jenkins; I'll take it in my bedroom."

Moments later she was standing in her bedroom with a towel wrapped loosely around her and a frown of exasperation on her face. She listened to the voice coming from the phone for a long minute, and then broke in abruptly. "Come off it, Adam! There's nothing in my contract that says I have to accept an acting job."

Since Dany was the least difficult of his models, Adam Hamilton's voice was more than a little surprised. "But, Danica—I thought you'd be pleased! This role could make you a star, for God's sake!"

Dany hung on to her patience with an effort. "I don't want to be a star, Adam. As of this morning, I am on vacation. That sportswear account isn't due to be shot until fall—so I'll see you then. Good-bye, Adam." She started to hang up the phone, and then said quickly, "Oh, and, Adam—"

"Yes?"

"Tell Mr. Spencer that I said good-bye." She cradled the phone gently and trailed bubbles all the way back to the tub.

Adam Hamilton smiled rather weakly at the fuming man on the other side of his desk. "She—uh—she doesn't want the part. . . ."

CHAPTER TWO

By late the next afternoon Dany was dividing her attention between the traffic leaving Portland and the ecstatic advances of her harlequin Great Dane. The huge dog was occupying the entire backseat of the small rental car, and only the cramped quarters had prevented him from attempting to sit in his mistress's lap.

"Stop it, Brutus!" Dany hastily warded off a tongue as large as a hand towel just in time to avoid running into the car in front of her. "For heaven's sake—settle down! I know you're happy to see me, and I'm happy to see you too. But neither one of us is going to make it home in one piece if you don't sit down and be quiet!"

She spared a moment to glance in the rearview mirror, smiling at the panting face of her four-footed friend. She hated leaving her pet in a kennel for weeks at a time, but there was nothing she could do about it until her career as a model was over. Just a few more months now . . .

Repeating the thought like a litany, Dany drove the fifty miles to the coast in record time. She was free! Free of modeling for a few months, free of the sound of a name she had come to hate: Bay Spencer.

The sun was dipping low over her beloved Pacific when Dany turned the car into the winding drive leading up to her house. She stopped the car before her house and turned the engine off, her eyes dwelling lovingly on the sprawling home. The weathered cedar siding blended perfectly with the dense growth of trees and shrubs surrounding the structure. It was a mountain aerie, a refuge from the prying world of lights and cameras to which she reluctantly belonged.

A couple from the nearby town of Sea Bend watched over the house and grounds whenever she was away, just as they had done for the past two years. Dany usually called them from New York to let them know when she would be coming home, but this time she had forgotten. Not that it would matter; Sam and Ellen Burke had probably already been to the house that week. The lawn, at least, appeared freshly mowed.

A gruff bark from the backseat recalled Dany's attention, and she hastily opened the car door and climbed out. "Okay, Brutus. We're home!" She shoved the driver's seat forward, and watched the dog struggle out of the car and dash madly around the small neatly trimmed lawn, apparently making sure that no other animal had invaded his domain in his absence.

With a happy smile Dany went around to get her cases out of the trunk, and then carried them into the house. Within moments she had gone through the house and flung open all the windows, trusting the brisk sea breeze to dispel the faintly musty smell of the rooms.

It was a three-bedroom home, though Dany had converted one of the bedrooms into a study shortly after she bought the house. The rooms were spacious and airy, the furnishings simple and comfortable. Plants abounded in

28

the den and kitchen. The entire ocean side of the house was floor-to-ceiling glass with patio doors leading from the den to a large wooden deck at the back of the house. When the drapes were opened, as they were now, there was a spectacular view of the ocean.

Dany sighed as she sank down on the comfortable sofa in front of the patio doors. She was home.

Three days later she had completely settled in. The house was spotless, the kitchen stocked with food after a hasty trip to the store, and she had unpacked completely —for the first time in nearly two months.

Dany was stretched out lazily on a lounge she had placed on the shaded side of the wooden deck. She would have preferred to lie in the sun, but since her creamy skin burned easily, she had long ago given up trying to cultivate the smoothly tanned look she so admired. She was wearing her favorite pair of cutoff jeans and a halter top; her copper-gold hair, released from the pins that normally kept it piled on top of her head, fell down her back in a silky mass to her waist.

A pitcher of iced tea and a half-filled glass sat on a small table beside the lounge; an unopened book lay in her lap. Sleepy green eyes watched the ocean for a while, and then slowly closed.

Dany awoke sometime later, not certain what had disturbed her, but aware that something had. She turned her head slowly to see a man leaning casually against the railing near the steps that led down to the private beach.

Wary green eyes moved consideringly over the jet-black, windblown hair, lowered to examine a face that was lean, deeply tanned, and hard as nails. Light blue eyes with all the warmth of the Arctic in the dead of winter returned her stare with no emotion whatsoever.

Dany tore her eyes from that uncomfortably piercing

gaze to take in the formidable breadth of shoulders beneath a knit sport shirt, then continued down the slim waist, over the narrow jean-clad hips and muscular legs, to the casual shoes.

If anything had been needed to spoil her vacation, it was the man standing a few short feet away. As her eyes slowly returned to the hard face, Dany acknowledged to herself that this was a man to be wary of. There was cold intelligence in the strangely light blue eyes, and both the six-foot height and the leanly powerful frame spoke of a strength not easily subdued. He looked confident and assured in a way that few men ever learn to be; at ease with himself and those around him—a man who took what he wanted, secure in the belief that he was fully capable of handling the consequences of his own actions.

And deep in the hidden part of herself Dany felt something quiver uncertainly as she looked at him. Instinct told her that she had never known a man such as this one, and yet he seemed oddly familiar to her.

Dany pushed the strange sensation away and, trying to ignore the suspicion in her mind, said pleasantly, "This is private property."

His smile was a mere twitch of the lips that in no way altered the cold blue eyes. "I'm aware of that, Miss Morgan." His voice was deep, and probably could be pleasant when he wanted it to be, but at the moment it was shedding icicles. "Unfortunately, since you seemed unable and unwilling to talk to me in New York, I was forced to come out here and add trespassing to all my other sins."

Her suspicion crystallized into reality. Dany abandoned her pleasant manner. "Mr. Spencer, can't you take no for an answer?"

"Not without an explanation," he responded curtly.

"The explanation is very simple: I have no desire to become an actress. Now, will you kindly get off my prop-

30

erty? Or shall I call my dog so that he can chase you away?"

One black brow rose in sardonic amusement. "I would hardly run from a toy poodle with ribbons on its ears, Miss Morgan."

Laughter, hastily suppressed, rose in Dany as she realized that he was referring to the tiny dog that she had posed with in several assignments last year. She didn't bother to correct his mistake; she simply whistled sharply for her pet.

She saw the flicker of surprise in the cold blue eyes when a deep-throated bark answered her call, and kept her gaze fixed on him as she heard her dog come through the open patio door and out onto the deck. He had been asleep inside the house. The huge dog stopped beside her lounge, a growl rumbling from his throat when he saw their visitor.

Dany rested a hand lightly on the bristling hairs at the back of her dog's neck. "This is Brutus," she said calmly. "And Brutus—like his namesake—has a tendency to do away with anyone he thinks the world would be better off without. Shall I tell him that we can easily dispense with your cheerful presence, Mr. Spencer?"

After a moment Spencer asked in a rueful voice, "Are you sure it's a dog? It looks more like a horse."

Dany felt an odd little flicker of shock when she saw amusement thaw his icy blue eyes, but she quickly overcame her impulse to relent toward him. "Whatever it is, it has teeth," she pointed out flatly. "And I can assure you that it isn't overly fond of strangers."

He sighed, and his eyes seemed to warm even more. "You and I got off on the wrong foot, Miss Morgan." Wry humor twisted the strong mouth into an oddly endearing lopsided smile. "Can we please start over? If you can spare me a few minutes of your time, I'd like to talk to you."

31

Dany had a sinking feeling that she could hardly refuse when the offer was put like that. Giving the dog a slight pat, she murmured, "Go lie down, Brutus." She watched the dog collapse obediently onto the deck, and then waved her guest to a nearby chair.

With one eye on the dog Spencer moved to sit down in the chair that she had indicated. Before he could speak, Dany asked the question foremost in her mind.

"How did you find out about this place? I'm not listed in the phone book, and the agency isn't allowed to give out my address."

His blue eyes seemed to drop a few degrees in temperature. "A friend of mine told me that Jason Carrington owned a beach house a few miles north of Sea Bend. After that, it was easy."

The rumors. Dany slipped into her cool, aloof mask. "I bought the house from Jason two years ago."

"Sure you did." His lips thinned slightly. "Just like you bought the penthouse in New York from him?"

Dany held her mask in place with an effort. "No, that belongs to Jason."

His gaze swept her slender body scathingly. "Like a few other things I could mention."

He might just as well have waved a red flag in front of a bull. Dany's cool composure shattered like ice flung against stone. She was on her feet in an instant, her vivid green eyes flashing with rage. He could not have known it, but part of her anger was directed inward; she was furious with herself because his words had the power to hurt her.

"I don't have to listen to this, Mr. Spencer! I don't know who you think you are, but I want you to get off my property!"

He rose slowly, ignoring the growling dog standing protectively by her side. With an odd gleam in his eyes he said

32

thoughtfully, "You're even more beautiful when you're angry. I knew you would be."

Disarmed by the note of sincerity in his voice, Dany stared at him speechlessly for a moment. It took an effort for her to say coldly, "I don't believe that you and I have anything to talk about."

"Miss Morgan, if I solemnly promise not to make any more uncalled-for remarks about your relationship with Carrington—which I admit is none of my business—will you give me another chance? I'm sorry if I offended you—"

"Yes," she interrupted flatly. "You did offend me. I don't like being insulted—especially in my own home."

Her remark seemed to surprise him for a moment, but he recovered quickly. "I am sorry, Miss Morgan. And I would like to talk to you about the film."

Eyeing him with a great deal of irritation, Dany sank back down on the lounge. "Mr. Spencer, I'm sorry that you were forced to fly out here," she sighed, "but that really wasn't my fault. I told Adam to tell you that I didn't want the part. He did tell you, didn't he?"

Spencer reseated himself and waited until Dany's furry guardian settled back onto the deck before replying. "Yes. I was in his office when he called you." The blue eyes were hooded as they watched her.

"Then why didn't you just accept it?"

He shrugged slightly. "Any other model would have given her right arm for that part; I was curious to find out why you refused it."

"And you traveled three thousand miles to find out?" She shook her head. "I find that hard to believe, Mr. Spencer."

He leaned forward suddenly, elbows resting on his knees, blue eyes intense. "This picture is very important to me, Miss Morgan. It's the last film I plan to actively

33

produce and I want it to be the best. With the right casting, and careful direction, it should take every award next year."

Frowning slightly, she murmured, "You're very sure of yourself, aren't you."

"I'm sure of the material I've been provided with," he responded tersely. "*A Time for Serena* is one of those rare books that comes along maybe once in a decade. It's powerful and real, and it moves people. Aurora Sanders should congratulate herself for having written a top-notch novel."

Dany dropped her lashes to veil her eyes, wondering in surprise why his praise had caused her to feel a sudden rush of gratification. Why should she care what he thought? "That may very well be, Mr. Spencer, but it doesn't explain why you flew three thousand miles to see me."

"Of course, it does," he said impatiently. "I came to see you in the hopes of persuading you to take the part of Serena. I think you'd be perfect."

"You've wasted a trip, then."

Ignoring her flat statement, he repeated, "You'd be perfect. The part would make you a star."

"I don't want to be a star!"

"Of course, you do; it's every little girl's dream," he told her with maddening patience.

Dany closed her eyes and counted silently to ten. When she opened her eyes, she found him staring at her with a puzzled expression on his face.

"Is something wrong, Miss Morgan?"

"I was counting," she replied carefully. "It keeps me from throwing things."

His blue eyes gleamed with sudden amusement. "Does my persistence irritate you, Miss Morgan?"

"Whatever gave you that idea?" There was a faint glint of responsive laughter in her own eyes.

Immediately he was serious. "I don't mean to badger you about the part, Miss Morgan. It's just that I can't picture anyone else as Serena."

"Then you'd better try." When he started to respond, she went on quickly, "I've read the novel, Mr. Spencer. In case you haven't noticed, Serena is a blonde. She's also several inches taller than I am, and she has blue eyes."

"So?"

Completely out of patience, she glared at him. "So there must be many actresses in Hollywood who look more like Serena than I do. Why pick on me?"

He nodded. "Physically, yes. However, I happen to see Serena as a redhead, and I mean to cast a redhead in the part."

"Not *this* redhead!" Dany snapped.

Calmly Spencer said, "I haven't told you how much the pay is." With a total lack of emotion in his voice, he quoted a figure that was staggering.

Dany gritted her teeth. "Not interested."

He promptly doubled the figure.

She stared at him for a moment, and then said very quietly, "You can go on adding zeros until doomsday if you want to, but it won't do any good. *I don't want the part!*"

He grinned suddenly and sat back in his chair. "Did you know that your eyes give off sparks when you're mad?"

Dany leaned her forehead wearily on one hand and murmured, "The man is impossible. Completely, utterly, totally—"

"—thoroughly, conclusively," he contributed helpfully.

"—altogether impossible!" she finished, lifting her head and glaring at him. "When it comes to the word *no,* you have a mental block!"

35

His grin was mocking. "Does that mean you don't want the part?" he asked innocently.

For the second time in the past five minutes Dany closed her eyes and counted—this time to twenty. She opened her eyes finally, and said with careful restraint, "That's what it means. I'm glad you finally got my drift."

"You don't want the part." He seemed to consider the matter, then asked, "Why not?"

After staring at his suspiciously grave expression for a moment, Dany turned her gaze to her sleeping pet. "Maybe if Brutus took a bite out of you—"

"You wouldn't dare!"

He was laughing openly now, and Dany was surprised to feel her pulse leap at the sound. Confused, she said hastily, "I certainly would! Don't ever dare a redhead!"

"I'll remember!" He sobered abruptly. "I would like to know your reasons though. I did, after all, come three thousand miles to find out what they were."

Still off balance, Dany told him the truth—or at least a part of it. "I don't want the exposure. I don't like being in the public eye, Mr. Spencer. Is that a good enough reason for you?"

"Not really." He looked skeptical. "If you don't want to be in the public eye, then why did you become a model in the first place?"

Dany was still bewildered by her response to this man, but some instinct prompted her to tell him why she had started modeling, and she did so without stopping to think. Meeting his eyes levelly, she said quietly, "My parents were killed in an accident five years ago. I was in college and didn't have the money to go on. A friend suggested that I try modeling, so I did. I signed a five-year contract with Adam Hamilton's agency." She was unaware of the sudden bitterness in her eyes. "I didn't realize what it would be like—the staring eyes, the probing ques-

36

tions, the complete lack of privacy. By the time I found out, it was too late. I was committed."

The expression in the hard blue eyes softened. "I'm sorry. I didn't know."

"Now you do." Horrified that she had exposed so much of herself to a stranger, Dany's voice was flat. "And now you have my reasons for turning down the part."

He nodded, heavy lids coming down to hide the expression in his eyes. "I can't argue with your reasons. Now, what am I supposed to do for the next three weeks?"

Startled, she forgot all about her embarrassment. "What?"

"I had allowed three weeks to convince you. Hamilton said you were stubborn," he explained calmly. "So what am I supposed to do for three weeks?"

Amused in spite of herself, Dany made her voice grave. "Take up a new hobby."

"Any suggestions?"

"They say bird-watching is nice."

"Too tame," he said seriously.

She thought for a moment. "Skydiving?"

"And get myself killed?" He shook his head. "No, thanks."

She chewed on her forefinger absently, then lifted it suddenly with an air of triumph. "I know! Surfing! There's the ocean—help yourself." Having thus disposed of the next three weeks of his time, she reached down to pick up her book from the deck beside her lounge and hid her face behind it.

There was a moment of silence. When he finally spoke, his voice quivered with laughter. "I think I've been dismissed!"

She peered over the book. "Are you still here? I thought you'd be surfing by now."

He looked pained. "Surfing? Come now, Miss Morgan. Surely you can come up with a better hobby than that."

Disappearing behind the book again, she responded with an irritatingly absent air. "Don't be ridiculous, Mr. Spencer. I can't be bothered with finding hobbies for bored producers. I'm on vacation." When the silence had stretched into minutes, she peered over the book again to find him staring at her. "Did you want something?"

"Funny you should ask." His tone was wry.

She lifted her eyebrows in a silent question and lowered the book, trying to keep her face expressionless.

"I want you to stop calling me Mr. Spencer. It's beginning to get on my nerves." He smiled the lopsided smile. "My friends call me Bay."

"Is that short for—"

"Baynard?" He grimaced slightly. "No, thank God. My mother named me after the San Francisco Bay."

She started to laugh. "You were named after a bay, and I was named after a star! I think that we both had very odd parents."

"Is that what *Danica* means? Star?"

"Morning star, actually. My mother was a romantic."

His blue eyes swept her thoughtfully. "She made a mistake. You're not a morning star."

"Oh? Then what am I?" she asked curiously.

Very softly, he replied, "You're a fiery sunset, warm and full of life. Or a brilliant sunrise, filled with promise."

"I think," she said carefully, "that you should have been a writer instead of a producer. You have a definite way with words." It took a great deal of effort for Dany to keep her voice light; his soft utterance had caused her heart to thump alarmingly. What on earth was wrong with her?

He laughed huskily. "It's the truth."

Dany felt uneasy beneath the sudden intensity of his

stare. She didn't want him to look at her like that. She didn't want to be forced to retreat behind her mask, but she had no choice. The habit of years, combined with the masculine interest in his eyes, drove her to hide herself from him. The polite mask slipped into place without her conscious awareness.

Immediately his gaze became narrow and searching. Before she could speak, he said quietly, "You didn't like what I said about you, did you?"

"I . . . don't like flattery." Her voice was very even.

He leaned forward to stare at her, the blue eyes darkened to indigo. "I have a lot of faults, Danica, but flattering isn't one of them. I'm demanding and critical, and blunt to the point of rudeness. If I say you're beautiful— and I do say that—then it's my honest opinion. Not flattery."

She stared into his eyes, relieved that he believed her sudden discomfort had been caused by his comments. She wasn't about to tell him that his words had disturbed her, but had not made her uncomfortable. The desire she had seen in his eyes had done that. She managed a slight smile. "I'll remember—Bay."

He grinned faintly. "Things are looking up. You didn't object when I called you Danica."

"No, but I'm going to now." Amusement filled her eyes when he looked surprised. "My friends call me Dany."

"Dany it is, then." His smile was friendly. "Would you be kind to a lonely producer, Dany, and have dinner with him?"

She glanced at her watch, surprised to find that it was after four o'clock. She lifted her eyes to study him uncertainly for a moment then asked, "Do you like pizza?"

"Love it."

She nodded and rose gracefully from the lounge. "Then why don't we eat here? I make terrific pizza."

He laughed as he followed her into the house. "You mean you can cook?"

She turned just inside the den to give him an offended look. "Just because I'm a model doesn't mean that I'm a lily of the field when it comes to everything else. I happen to love cooking."

"Well, don't get all hot and bothered about it," he commented mildly, watching as she dropped her book on the coffee table. "How was I supposed to know?" He felt a nudge against his legs, and stepped aside hastily as Brutus came into the room. "Does he go everywhere with you?"

Dany looked blank for a minute and then realized that he was talking about her pet. She smiled as she watched the large dog collapse in front of the fireplace. "He does when I'm home. When I'm working, he has to stay in a kennel."

She headed for the kitchen, feeling her neck tingle slightly as she entered the cheery yellow-and-orange room. Frowning, she wondered what had caused the strange sensation. Rubbing the back of her neck absently, she bent to remove a pizza pan from the cabinet by the stove.

"Can I help?"

Straightening, she turned to find him lounging in the doorway, watching her quizzically. With that charmingly lopsided smile, he said, "I'm not so bad in a kitchen myself."

She surveyed him critically. "How are your salads?"

"I toss a mean salad," he replied seriously.

Emerald eyes glittering with amusement, she waved toward the refrigerator. "Everything's in there. Go to it!"

Somewhat to her surprise, she found that Bay *did* toss a mean salad. By the time she was grating cheese for the pizza topping, he was setting the tossed salad in the refrig-

40

erator. They had worked together in complete harmony, and Dany was surprised to find herself at ease with him. The thought had barely crossed her mind when her neck tingled.

"You know, you're awfully small to be a model."

The sudden comment came from directly behind her, and Dany jumped, startled. Looking over her shoulder, she found him almost too close for comfort. Adopting a light voice, she said, "I haven't heard any complaints."

Bay moved to lean against the counter at her side. "Oh, I wasn't complaining. I was just thinking that you're unusual in more ways than one. Do you only wear makeup when you're working?"

She stared at him, caught off guard. "Well, yes, usually. Why? Is my nose shiny?"

"At the moment," he responded gravely, "it's smudged with flour."

Dany sternly controlled an impulse to rub her nose, and wrinkled it instead. "A good cook always smears a little of the ingredients on herself."

He grinned. "Where did you hear that?"

"My mother." She started sprinkling grated cheese over the pizza. "Whenever Mama came out of the kitchen, she always looked as though she'd gone ten rounds with a bag of flour and lost the fight."

He shook with silent laughter. "Really? I'd like to have met her. What was your father like?"

"Patient, mostly." Dany's busy fingers stilled; she stared into space with a reflective frown. "He was an English professor with a great deal of respect for education. He and Mama were complete opposites in temperament. Mama was bubbly and enthusiastic; Daddy was quiet and thoughtful. Together, they seemed . . . complete."

As if sensing that talk of her parents was making Dany

feel sad, Bay changed the subject abruptly. "You said that you had signed a five-year contract with Hamilton's agency. What do you plan to do after that?"

Dany started to reply, "Write, of course," but quickly stopped herself. "Oh, I don't know. I've thought about going back to college. I'd like to get my degree."

"What were you studying?"

"I majored in English literature." She moved to place the pizza in the oven, then straightened with a slight smile. "Not that there's any great demand for English degrees these days."

Heavy lids dropped suddenly to veil Bay's eyes. "Who suggested that you try modeling, Dany?"

The unexpected question threw her for a moment. She stared at his hooded eyes, some instinct telling her that he already knew the answer to his question. "Jason," she replied quietly.

His mouth twisted strangely. "That's what I thought."

All at once, Dany was conscious of an intense desire to tell Bay the truth about her relationship with Jason. She didn't stop to wonder why she wanted him to know; it just seemed important somehow. "Bay"—she reached out to touch his arm lightly, and then let her hand drop—"you were talking about your faults a while ago. Well, I have faults too. But I don't lie."

He nodded slowly, watching her.

"No matter what you think, no matter what you've heard," she said evenly, "I am not—and never have been—Jason's mistress. We're friends. Just friends."

"The penthouse?"

She easily understood the cryptic question. "The penthouse is for Jason's business associates. Since I'm rarely in New York, it would be a waste of money to rent an apartment or stay in a hotel, so I stay at the penthouse. Alone, except for the houseman."

He smiled slightly. "Empty rumors?"

Dany's answering smile was wry. "Empty rumors. No one-night stands, no weekend flings, no five-year affair. Just a warm friendship."

After a moment he said quietly, "I promise not to mention it again."

Relieved, she said lightly, "Good. Now—make yourself useful and set the table!"

Once more the conversation was friendly and uncomplicated. But Dany was aware of a weight settling over her that had not been there before. It mattered to her what Bay thought. For some reason beyond her comprehension it mattered. And she was convinced that he had not believed her. He still thought that she was Jason's mistress.

Bay raved about the pizza, saying that it was the best he had ever eaten. He paid her so many lavish compliments on her cooking that she was soon flustered and begging him to stop.

They shared the cleaning-up chores, talking together casually about unimportant things. Danica had been faintly surprised to find that he was staying at Sea Bend's smallest inn, confessing that she had expected him to be at a larger and more luxurious hotel. Bay had immediately taken exception to the remark, declaring that he liked small inns, and besides, it was right on the beach. When she had asked what that had to do with it, he explained that the inn was just a short walk from her house, and that it was quicker to walk along the beach.

She watched later as he strolled off up the beach, heading for the inn. He had gravely asked her permission to come back tomorrow, and Dany had granted it with equal gravity.

She wanted to see him again.

CHAPTER THREE

Dany was more than a little confused when the realization presented itself to her. She wanted to see Bay again . . . but why? Staring after his retreating figure, she rubbed her arms absently in the late evening chill. She was standing out on the deck, and as Bay disappeared into the distance, she turned her gaze to the darkly shimmering ocean.

Why? Why did she want to see him again? Was it because of that odd sense of recognition she had felt when she had first seen him? As if she knew him in some way? Or was it because he made her laugh, because he made her feel like a *person* instead of just a face or figure?

Dany leaned on the deck railing, frowning slightly as she stared out over the water. After a few moments thought, she finally decided that she wanted to see him again because he made her feel like a person. He was casual and companionable, and she liked that.

In some surprise, Dany realized then that she couldn't recall having a single male friend during the past five years. She had met countless men, but none had gotten close enough to form a friendship. Oh, there was Jason, of course. But Jason was more like an uncle—or even a father. She had never regarded him as a "male friend."

She had dated in high school and college, but the only lasting impression of those days were her memories of heated arguments and wrestling matches. The "new morality." . . .

With a slight shiver, not entirely caused by the chilly breeze, Dany went inside the house and closed the glass door behind her, shutting out her memories along with the cool night air. The past was no longer important; it was the present that disturbed her now.

She wasn't completely certain that she wanted to get involved with Bay Spencer, even on a casually friendly basis. He seemed to have the knack of slipping beneath her guard, and that bothered her. It also bothered her that he had apparently given up his intention of persuading her to accept the role of Serena in his film. It seemed . . . out of character somehow.

Still frowning, Dany sat down on the sofa and absently patted Brutus when he came over to rest his massive head in her lap. Still thinking about Bay, she made up her mind to tread very carefully where he was concerned. Her instinct had already warned her that he was a man to be wary of. . . .

It was late the next morning when Bay reappeared at the beach house. Approaching as silently as he had the day before, he climbed the steps to the deck, finding Dany seated cross-legged on the deck and staring solemnly at a drooping Boston fern placed in front of her. Bay leaned against the railing and folded his arms across his chest, his mouth quivering with amusement as he listened to her talking gravely to the plant.

"I'm home now," she was saying seriously, "so you can

straighten up. I know it wasn't nice of me to leave you all alone, but I do have a job, you know. But I'll be home all summer, so you won't be alone."

She reached up almost absently to rub the back of her neck, and then stiffened slightly as she slowly turned her head to see her silent observer. "Oh . . . hello."

"Good morning." Bay nodded toward the plant. "What's his name?"

"Oscar . . . and stop making fun of me!" Her glare was compounded of irritation and embarrassment.

He started laughing. "You know, Dany, you're not at all what I expected. You have a temper and a sense of humor. Your dog is bigger than you are; you talk to your plants; you cook like a dream." The laughter was gone now; his stare was assessing. Thoughtfully he murmured, "No, you're not at all what I expected."

Dany got to her feet slowly, her embarrassment over having been caught talking to a plant forgotten. His probing gaze was making her more than a little nervous, and she slipped behind her mask without even thinking about it. "And just what did you expect?" she asked rather dryly.

"I'm not really sure." His blue eyes swept the slender length of her body, taking in the faded jeans and yellow knit top. "A glamorous model, I suppose."

Her emerald eyes flashed with bitterness. "You're no exception. Most people seem to expect that."

A faint, disturbed frown crossed his face; the blue eyes darkened to indigo. "I'm sorry, Dany. I didn't realize that it bothered you so much."

Her mask of aloofness remained in place. "You're hardly responsible for the opinions of others. Only your own." In spite of her lack of expression there was a slight emphasis placed on the last three words.

His frown remained. "My own opinion," he said slowly,

47

"is that there's more to Danica Morgan than the surface shows."

This had to stop; they were both too serious. "There's more to all of us than the surface shows," she responded calmly. "Yourself, for instance."

He looked startled. "What about me?"

"I've heard a lot about you. I expected you to be a six-foot dragon breathing fire. Of course, you're not. So that must be beneath the surface."

Bay stared at her completely expressionless face for a moment and then burst out laughing. "Remind me not to cross swords with you—you're lethal!"

Dany allowed a slight smile to cross her face. "I'm glad you're amused. I was serious."

He stopped laughing. "You're kidding. You mean, you *have* heard rotten things about me?"

"Such arrogance," she mocked softly. "Did you expect everything to be good?"

"Well, I didn't expect to be thought of as a dragon. Did you really hear that?" He sounded as if he wasn't quite sure whether she was serious or not.

"To tell you the truth," she responded in a confiding tone, "if I *had* believed everything I heard, I would have expected the Devil himself. But I took all the rumors with a grain of salt."

Bay's eyes widened slightly. "Good Lord," he muttered. "I'm going to have to talk to the studio's publicity agent."

"Why?" Dany's tone was innocent. "He's only doing his job. He's getting you talked about."

"Yes, but—" Blue eyes narrowed in sudden suspicion. "I get the feeling," he said in a conversational voice, "that you're having a little bit of fun at my expense."

She gave him a wounded look. "Why would I do that? I've been telling you nothing but the truth."

48

"And just exactly what have you heard?"

Dany chewed on her forefinger with a thoughtful frown. "Actually," she said slowly, "I don't remember *exactly* what was said. I just remember gaining the impression that you were a monster. So I pictured you as a dragon."

"Dany . . ." he began dangerously.

She started laughing. "Honestly! Needless to say, I wasn't very happy when the dragon decided to pay me a visit."

"And now?" His eyes were twinkling slightly.

"Now . . . I'm reserving judgment." There was a smile lurking in her own eyes. "Purely academic curiosity, I assure you. The dragon may yet have some redeeming feature."

Very seriously he responded, "I should certainly hope so. Even the worst of the beasts have something to recommend them."

Dany frowned slightly. "What do you lump together in that 'beast' category? Snakes, for instance, have absolutely nothing to recommend them as far as I'm concerned."

Gravely he said, "They get around pretty well, considering they don't have any legs."

"That," she pointed out, "can hardly be considered a redeeming feature. Especially when one is being chased by a snake."

He looked thoughtful. "Well, sometimes their venom is used as a cure."

"A cure for what?"

"Damned if I know. Another snakebite, I guess."

Dany was enjoying the silly conversation. It told her a great deal about Bay's sense of humor. "I'll take your word for it. What about spiders?"

"What about them?"

"I'm putting them in the beast category. What do they have to recommend them?"

49

"They spin webs," he offered.

"You'll have to do better than that."

He considered for a moment, and then lifted a triumphant finger. "They eat other spiders!"

"Do they?" Dany asked involuntarily.

"Black widows do. When the females no longer have—uh—any use for the males, they eat them."

"Oh." Dany shuddered slightly. "Yuk." She thought for a minute, and then lifted an eyebrow. "I suppose it's their way of ensuring fidelity."

"Or their next meal."

Dany stared at him. "Bats."

"I beg your pardon?"

"Find something good about bats." She was desperately trying to keep from laughing.

Bay looked as though he were having the same problem. "Radar," he said tersely. Then an expression of uncertainty crossed his face. "Or maybe it's sonar. . . ."

It was more than Dany could stand. With a gasp she burst out laughing. "Lord, you're stubborn! If I had suggested warts, you probably would have found something good about *them*!"

"I'll tell you something good about them—I don't have any!" He was laughing every bit as hard as she was. He finally sobered long enough to say teasingly, "As fascinating as this conversation is, it isn't what I came over here to talk about."

Dany wiped her eyes, asking shakily, "And what was that?"

"Lunch," he replied succinctly.

In mock disgust she said, "Listen to the man! All he can think about is food!"

"It's better than what you think about." He started laughing again. "Dragons, snakes, spiders, bats, and warts! A regular witch's caldron!"

"Touché!" Dany tried to straighten out her face and found, to her surprise, that the mask had flown long before. "What were you saying about lunch?"

"I haven't said much of anything yet." He grinned at her. "I was planning to ask if you'd like to go on a picnic."

"Well, that depends."

"On what?"

"On who brings the food."

"After the shameless way you called me a dragon, I should make you bring it." The blue eyes glittered with amusement. "However, since I happen to be a gentleman, I will take care of that little item."

"In that case—lead on."

"You're supposed to say 'Lay on, Macduff'."

She looked him over with an exaggerated measuring eye. "Ah! I see I'll have to catch up on my reading."

"No classical list? Dany, I'm surprised at you!"

"Hey! You're talking to an English lit major, I'll have you know. I'm just a little rusty, that's all."

He chuckled softly. "Well, Miss English Lit Major, if you'll go grab a sweater and exchange those fuzzy things on your feet for a pair of rubber-soled shoes, we can be on our way."

"Those 'fuzzy things,'" she informed him haughtily, "happen to be house slippers."

"They certainly ruin your image of a glamorous model," he said teasingly.

"Glamorous models are only human, you know. If you could see what we have to do—for hours at a time—wearing six-inch heels, you'd understand why most of us go barefoot or wear fuzzy slippers when we have time off."

He laughed. "Point taken. Now, go get ready, or I'll have to picnic all by my lonesome."

"Yes, sir!" She picked up her plant and went inside the house, laughing quietly. She collected a sweater from her

51

bedroom, put on a pair of tennis shoes, then ordered Brutus to stay put and firmly shut the glass door in his disappointed canine face. (He tended to have a disastrous effect on picnics.)

She found Bay waiting for her by the steps. With a gallant flourish he indicated that she should precede him, and Dany took the cue as if she had been born on the stage. Head high and an aloof smile on her face, she tossed her sweater over an arm as if it were a mink stole, and started down the steps with all the dignity of a queen.

Halfway to the bottom of the steps she heard Bay chuckling behind her. "Hollywood lost a great talent when you decided not to become an actress, Dany— you're a natural."

Dany abandoned her dignified pose, and started to laugh. "A natural ham, you mean. From the school of melodramatic posturing!"

As they reached the beach Bay took her arm and began to lead her in the general direction of the inn he was staying at. "Oh, I don't know," he said judiciously. "With a bit of work you'd do great. Besides, they say the old school of acting is coming back."

Dany shot him a look of mock horror. "What? No more talkies?"

"Not *that* old!" he objected with a laugh.

Firmly she said, "It doesn't matter, because I'm not going to become an actress. No matter which school takes precedence."

He cocked a questioning brow at her. "Last word?"

"Last word." Her voice was definite.

He appeared to take this philosophically, and a companionable silence stretched between them for some minutes. Finally, just as they were rounding the bend that would put them within sight of the inn, and the small pier that marked its northern boundary, Dany asked a rather dry question.

"By the way, is this picnic to be on land or at sea?"

He sent her a sidelong teasing glance. "Quick, aren't you?"

"I try," she said modestly. Then, when he made a threatening gesture, she laughed. "Well, what else could I think? I would hardly need rubber-soled shoes on the beach!"

"True." He grinned at her. "Since your brilliant mind has already worked it out, I'll give in and tell you that we are having our picnic at sea."

Her eyes gleamed with amusement. "Don't tell me—let me guess. You found us a pair of kayaks!"

Shaking his head sorrowfully, he remarked, "You have a very suspicious nature."

They rounded the bend just then, stopping as they came upon the small pier. Normally there were several small boats tied up there, but today there was only one. It was a sixteen-foot sailboat that was obviously the pride and joy of its owner: every inch of the small vessel gleamed.

Dany looked at Bay with faint respect. "How in the world did you manage to pry Mr. Martin's boat away from him?" she asked, referring to the owner of the inn, a man who had earned his reputation as a difficult man.

"He offered to lend it to me."

Dany smiled at him sweetly. "I don't believe you."

Bay looked offended. "Are you calling me a liar?"

"Yes."

"He *did* offer to lend it to me!" Bay glared at her, but when she refused to back down, he gave up. "Well . . . he offered to lend it to me *after* I asked to borrow it. *And* after I convinced him that I wouldn't run it aground."

Dany tapped one foot patiently and waited.

Bay heaved an exasperated sigh. "All right! He *rented* it to me after I convinced him I could pay for the damn thing if I *did* run it aground! Satisfied?"

She started laughing. "You might have said so in the first place."

"I was trying to impress you." His smile was crooked. "Considering how crotchety old Martin is, I hoped you'd think I had winning ways."

Dany walked out onto the pier and tossed her sweater into the sailboat before responding. With a faint smile she said, "Oh, I knew that already. I was planning on a nice relaxing vacation, and here you've got me crewing for you on a sailboat. Not just anybody could have done that."

He had followed her to the boat, and now stood with his hands resting on his hips as he studied her thoughtfully. "I get the feeling you've been around boats."

She was peering over the side to inspect a wicker hamper. "Are you kidding?" she asked absently. "I was born on the coast of Maine—I practically grew up on a boat."

He waited until she turned back to him before asking rather dryly, "Any other hidden talents?"

She looked surprised. "What do you mean?"

With mock gravity he began to count off points on his fingers. "Beautiful, intelligent, sense of humor, gourmet cook, selective in your choice of companions"—Dany smiled at that one—"and an expert on boats. Any other hidden talents?"

Her smile deepened. "Just one: I swim like a fish." She laughed at his pained expression. "Tough luck—you won't be able to save me from near drowning at sea!"

He made a half-humorous grimace. "I forgot one item for my list."

"Oh? What's that?"

"You also read minds."

Dany laughed again. "It was obvious. But there's something you forgot—you got your roles reversed. The dragon is the one the heroine is being saved *from*. He never does the saving!"

He sighed. "I think we'd better shove off. If you get back on the subject of dragons, I'll starve to death."

"Aye, aye, skipper!"

Within moments, they had cast off and were under way. The ocean was choppy so close to shore, and they were forced to use the paddles to get out into the smoother water. After several minutes of steady work Bay moved forward to raise the sails while Dany took control of the boat. She was pleased to see that he took her at her word and made no effort to instruct her on the intricacies of sailing. They worked together like a familiar team.

Balancing easily on the starboard side of the small vessel, Bay pointed toward the north of their position. "There's a cove not far from here," he called to Dany. "Once we really catch the wind, make for that clump of trees up there. The cove's just beyond that."

Dany, sitting in the stern with one hand firmly on the tiller, nodded her understanding and watched him. Something tugged at her, an awareness of him as a man, but she hastily pushed the sensation away. She didn't know him. Not yet.

Quite suddenly she remembered something her father had told her once. The elder Morgan had been a sailing enthusiast, and had often taken his family out on their small boat. As if it were yesterday, Dany heard her father's words.

"If you ever want to see a man's true nature, Dany, dump him into the briny unexpectedly—provided, of course, that he can swim!"

She felt the wind snatch at the sails. At the exact same moment a demon seemed to take control of her. Her hand moved suddenly on the tiller. The little craft responded instantly, heeling over into the wind. The boom swung across smoothly.

Bay was caught completely by surprise. The sudden change in course threw him off balance, and the swinging boom completed the job. With a resounding whack it struck him across the middle of his back and propelled him into the sea.

Torn between laughter and horror at her own actions, Dany quickly brought the boat back around and headed toward the dark head bobbing in the water. When she was nearly there, she scrambled forward to drop the sails. The small vessel drifted slowly without the wind at its back, until it reached the man who was stoically treading water.

When he made no effort to climb into the boat, Dany leaned over with a rather weak smile. "I—uh—forgot to say 'coming about.'"

His face was completely impassive. "*Did* you? And here I was thinking that I just hadn't heard you say it."

Dany tried to fight the smile tugging at the corners of her mouth. "I didn't know that dragons could swim," she offered, hoping that he wasn't really angry.

"Is that why you dumped me? Curiosity?"

"I *didn't* dump you!" she fired up immediately. "It was a mistake, that's all. A tiny mistake!"

He continued to stare at her expressionlessly.

"Well," she murmured finally, "maybe it was—just possibly—an irresistible impulse. . . ."

"Dany," he said dangerously, "if I weren't a gentleman —"

"But you are!" she interrupted hastily. "Never forget that you are! And it wouldn't be gentlemanly to try and get even, now, would it?"

He burst out laughing. "You little devil! Here—give me a hand."

56

Dany started to obey, and then quickly drew back. "Oh, no, you don't! I've been had by that trick before!"

His eyes were very bright, the cobalt glitter a combination of irritation and amusement. "Ah! You do read minds, after all!" The boat tilted as he heaved himself aboard. He sat there for a moment, water pooling around him as he stared consideringly at her. "I ought to pick you up and throw you in just to teach you a lesson," he threatened.

Dany smiled at him uncertainly. "Couldn't you just forgive and forget? Please?"

He seemed to take forever to come to a decision, and Dany sighed with relief when he grinned faintly and nodded. "I'll let you get away with it . . . this time."

After that the rest of the day went smoothly. They sailed the boat to the cove that Bay had mentioned and had a wonderful time. The hamper that the inn had provided was amply stocked with chicken, potato salad, cheese, rolls, and a bottle of wine. After they had eaten all they could hold, they took turns fishing with a cane pole Bay unearthed from the storage locker. In spite of a bit of chicken used as bait, they didn't catch anything, but they enjoyed trying.

The sun was hanging low over the Pacific when they walked back up the beach after tying the sailboat at the pier. Bay broke the companionable silence as they reached the steps leading up to Dany's house.

"I have some phone calls to make, so I'll say good night now."

Dany turned to him with a smile. "It was a wonderful day. Thank you."

"Thank *you*," he responded gravely. Without warning he leaned over and kissed her lightly. "Even for the dunking."

Still surprised by the kiss, Dany laughed. "I'm sorry about that—really!"

"I'll pay you back someday," he promised casually. He started to turn away from her and then paused. "See you tomorrow?"

She smiled and nodded. "Tomorrow." She watched until he was out of sight and then climbed the steps to the deck. Letting Brutus out of the house, she scolded him affectionately for his boisterous greeting, and then wandered over to lean against the railing of the deck. The ocean had never seemed so blue; the air had never seemed so crisp and clean. It was as if she were seeing everything clearly for the first time.

She felt . . . *alive*. Really alive for the first time in years. She realized then that she had not only hidden from the public eye since she had become a model; she had hidden from herself as well.

She had come of age in a business that was highly competitive and sometimes brutally insensitive, and the experience had scarred her. She had learned to hide her feelings so completely that, after a time, she had begun to hide them even from herself. She had been half asleep for years, preferring a shadowy existence to harsh reality.

But now she was wide-awake. Something had happened. She wasn't quite sure what it was, but instinct told her that it had a great deal to do with the man who had just left.

In some manner beyond her understanding he had managed to strip away her inner mask. She had seen herself through his eyes—and she had not been displeased with what she had seen. She was a normal woman—not frigid, as some men had claimed. She had not turned away coldly from Bay's kiss, had she? Of course not!

It had been . . . rather pleasant. . . .

* * *

It didn't take Dany more than a few days to realize that either the rumors about Bay Spencer had been completely false, or else he was showing her a side of himself that no one had ever seen. He was friendly and charming, teasing her until she was helpless with laughter. He seemed content to treat her as a friend, making no attempt to begin a more intimate relationship with her.

At first Dany was pleased with the undemanding friendship. It was a novel situation for her, and she enjoyed being able to spend time with a man who asked nothing more than her company. She began to spend less and less time behind her polite mask, only retreating when he inadvertently came too close.

But as the days passed, Dany began to wonder if there was something wrong with her. The light, almost brotherly kisses he bestowed on her every night left her unsatisfied, and she tossed and turned in her bed with an ache that would not leave her in peace. Wryly aware of her own perverse attitude, she nonetheless wished that he would at least let her know he found her desirable.

Before, she had always shied away from a physical relationship with a man, but she found herself strangely drawn to Bay. His teasing smile made her feel oddly light-headed, and his slightest touch produced in her a longing that both surprised and shocked her. She didn't understand her reaction to the man she had once professed to hate, and the fact that the attraction was apparently one-sided did nothing to help her state of mind.

She tried to figure out why she was so attracted to him. He was not handsome in the accepted sense; his features were rugged, his blue eyes sometimes hard and too often probing. His lean, powerful body moved with a peculiar, catlike grace, but it wasn't only that that caused her heart to pound whenever she saw him.

Chemistry? A totally physical reaction to an attractive

man? But she had met many men in her life who had been classically handsome, and none of them had stirred so much as a flutter in her pulse. Sheer charm? No. She had met men who had the ability to charm the Devil out of his left horn, and they had made no impression. Humor? Wit? No. She had known men who could easily rouse her to laughter, men who had held her attention with their witty conversation. Intelligence? Certainly he was intelligent, and she responded to that.

It was a mental as well as physical reaction. He made her feel special. Whenever she was with him, she always enjoyed herself—no matter what they did. She was never bored, never conscious of time dragging.

What was there about him that tugged so irresistibly at her mind and her senses?

Dany discovered the answer to her questions at the end of the second week. She was lying on a beach blanket and lifted her head to watch Bay coming toward her after a swim. His tanned body glistened with water; his black hair gleamed wetly in the sunlight. The hard muscled flesh and pantherlike walk gave him the look of some pagan god, and she felt her heart speed up almost painfully.

Grateful for the shield of her sunglasses, Dany smiled, handing him a towel as he dropped down beside her on the large blanket. Without sitting up, she watched as he dried his arms and chest, suddenly aware of what it was that attracted her to him physically.

There was a suggestion of blatant sensuality about him, an almost animal magnetism, fiery and primitive. At times like this—without cumbersome clothing and all the other trappings of civilization—he became an elemental force as powerful and unyielding as the ocean he had just left.

Dany let her shielded gaze wander over his body, watching muscles ripple along his arms and back as he dried his legs. Fine black hair covered his chest and arrowed down his flat stomach, disappearing beneath the waistband of his black swimming trunks. His powerfully muscled legs were long and tanned, lightly covered with the fine black hair.

Slowly Dany's eyes moved back to his face. It was a hard face, certainly, but one filled with character. There was strength and determination there, and the faintly sensual curve of his lower lip only hinted at the boiling caldron she was suddenly certain lurked beneath the veneer of civilization.

With a soundless gasp Dany tore her eyes away from his absorbed face and stared up at the sky. She felt strangely shocked to realize that her attraction to this man was based on something so primitive. But it was. With an instinct as old as time, her body responded to the savage it sensed within him. And that response was as instinctive and inevitable as the way her mind responded to his intelligence and humor.

She loved him. Like a bolt out of the blue the knowledge hit her, sending tingles of sudden awareness along her nerve endings. She loved him!

And now she knew why she had felt a fleeting shock of recognition when they had first met. She *had* known him. He was every hero she had ever devised for her books. He was the faceless man in the dreams that had haunted her for years.

He was her destiny.

CHAPTER FOUR

A touch on her shoulder just then caused Dany to nearly jump out of her skin. She turned her head to see Bay smiling crookedly at her.

"You're beginning to turn pink," he observed. "I think we'd better go inside."

Murmuring an agreement, Dany scrambled to her feet and hastily shrugged into her thigh-length terry beach robe, wondering irritably why she suddenly felt naked in the tiny bikini. God knew, she had modeled briefer ones for fashion layouts. And then she became aware of the tingle on her neck, and she knew why she felt naked.

Bay was watching her. And now that she had realized how she felt about him, she was painfully conscious of every move he made, every glance. She had felt flashes of that awareness before—but only flashes. When he had touched her, when she had watched him walking toward her, she had become briefly aware of the aura of sensuality surrounding him. But then she had always shunted the realization aside without really acknowledging it to herself.

Unfortunately for her peace of mind, she couldn't do that now. Bay was all man, and her body responded to that fact with every nerve it possessed. And she was helpless to prevent the betraying flush that rose to her cheeks.

Bending swiftly, she picked up two corners of the blanket and began to shake it vigorously, hoping that Bay wouldn't notice her red face. But of course he did.

"You got more sun that I thought." He was frowning slightly as he gazed at her face. "We shouldn't have stayed out so long."

Dany kept her attention on the blanket she was folding. Determinedly offhand, she said, "It'll be all right. I'm never as burned as I look."

"I hope not." He gathered the remainder of their things and followed her toward the house. "If it starts to bother you later, just let me know. There's a very good brand of first-aid cream that works wonders."

Dany merely nodded and climbed the steps to the deck in silence. She was tempted to ask him if the cream he spoke of worked as well internally; she was very much afraid that she was going to be badly burned somewhere near her heart. She was head-over-heels in love with a man who had shown no more than a friendly interest in her, and already she was aching inside.

When they went inside the house, Dany pulled off her sunglasses and murmured, "I'll go and change. The last of that beer you brought is in the refrigerator, if you want it." She was desperate to get away from him long enough to sort out her thoughts.

"Okay," he responded casually. "Take your time."

Dany beat a hasty retreat down the hallway, nearly holding her breath until the bedroom door was safely closed behind her. Fool! she scolded herself sharply. You're behaving like an idiot!

Leaving her hair up, she quickly took a shower to wash

away the salt of an earlier swim and then dressed in jeans and a bulky sweater, anticipating the late afternoon chill of this time of year. She left off her bra, since the flesh of her shoulders was a little burned. Thrusting her feet into the fuzzy house slippers that Bay had teased her about, she pushed the sleeves of her sweater up to her elbows and went over to the dresser to take down her hair.

While she brushed her hair Dany thought carefully about her relationship with Bay. It was, at least for the moment, based on easy companionship. They got along well, without the complications that physical intimacy could conceivably bring.

Her hand stopped in midstroke. Was that what she wanted? An affair? Almost violently, the hand continued its movements. No. She definitely did not want an affair. To her mind, love had always been a special thing, not to be tarnished by the casualness of a one-night stand or a summer fling.

And she loved Bay. She wanted to spend the rest of her life with him. But what did he want? Since her withdrawal that first day, he had never given the slightest sign that he even desired her—let alone felt anything deeper and more lasting.

Dany sighed as she placed the brush on the dresser. Since she wasn't about to throw herself at him, she knew that she would just have to wait and see what happened between them. They would have at least another week; Bay had told her that he had allowed three weeks to "convince" her to take that role in his film. One more week . . .

When she entered the den a few moments later, Bay was sprawled on the sofa with his eyes closed and a beer can propped on his flat stomach. Staring down at his recumbent body, Dany noted that he had changed back into the clothes he had been wearing earlier in the day: dark slacks and a blue shirt. The sleeves were folded back to reveal his tanned forearms, and she felt that disturbing prickle of awareness again as she looked at the bronzed skin. When one blue eye opened to stare up at her, she said the first thing that came into her mind.

"I hope you took off those wet trunks."

Both eyes opened then, and darkened with amusement as he gazed at her suddenly flushed cheeks. "My God," he said softly, "you're blushing. I thought that was a lost art."

Trying to ignore her heated face, Dany frowned at him and wondered what had possessed her to mention those damn trunks. "Well, now you know . . . it isn't."

He started to laugh, but quickly sobered when her frown deepened. Very gravely, he said, "I did take the trunks off, so now you don't have to worry that I'll catch cold."

She wasn't fooled by the gravity, since his blue eyes were gleaming with amusement, but she decided to ignore the whole thing. "Do you like spaghetti?"

He looked startled. "As a matter of fact, it's a favorite of mine. Why?"

She started for the kitchen. "Because I have a recipe that never fails."

He sat up quickly, catching the beer can before it could spill its contents all over him. Staring after her retreating figure, he asked suspiciously, "Never fails? To do what?"

She paused at the kitchen door long enough to smile gently over her shoulder at him. "Never fails to cause indigestion."

She heard him groan as she continued into the kitchen, and laughed as she began to gather together the ingredients she needed. Bay followed her moments later, and the next hour or so was spent in the same atmosphere of easy

66

companionship that they had shared for the past two weeks.

Bay insisted on doing the cleaning up after the meal, declaring that anyone who had made such a delicious sauce shouldn't have to do anything so mundane as clean up the mess. Dany's arguments lacked force, so she wasn't really surprised to find herself seated on the rug before a roaring fire with a cup of coffee on the stone hearth within easy reach.

She pulled a pillow from the sofa and placed it behind her, smiling faintly as she listened to Bay whistling in the kitchen. Leaning back lazily, she stared into the fire and allowed her body and mind to relax totally.

Much later, she stirred slightly as she felt that odd little tingle on the back of her neck. Frowning slightly, she looked over her shoulder to find him watching her with strange intensity. Before she could move or speak, he was beside her on the thick rug, one hand reaching gently to touch her flushed cheek.

The moment his fingers made contact with her soft skin, Dany felt a sudden heat envelop her—a heat that owed little to the bright orange flames flickering in the fireplace. She felt confused and uncertain, her green eyes shimmering darkly as she looked up at him.

In a soft musing voice Bay said, "You're a beautiful woman, Dany. When your hair is falling down your back, and you aren't wearing any makeup, you have the innocence and gentleness of a child. And then you look at me with those seductive, bewitching green eyes, and suddenly you aren't a little girl any longer."

Dany caught her breath on a gasp when one of his fingers moved to touch her small straight nose and then lowered to trace slowly the delicate outline of her lips. The almost reverent caress caused her pulse to quicken, half in alarm and half in nervous excitement, and she knew that she was dangerously vulnerable because of her love for this man. She fought a desire to touch the lean, hard face so close to her own; fear of the unknown made her stiffen and start to draw away from him.

But it was too late.

With a muffled groan he pulled her into a crushing embrace, his lips finding hers with fiery desire. Completely unprepared for the savage assault on her senses, Dany felt her world reel, and her response was instinctive. Her arms moved up to circle his neck, her lips parted beneath the insistent pressure of his.

Bay drew her even closer, her instant response wrenching another groan from him. One hand tangled in her copper-gold hair as the other moved caressingly up her spine. He seemed hungry for her, his lips plundering the sweetness of hers with an almost desperate need. Lowering her to the rug, he half covered her body with his, and she made no move to stop him.

Dany felt lost in a vortex of molten desire; her ability to think had clearly vanished. She had never been held or touched by a man the way that Bay was holding and touching her, and when his rough hand found the softness of her breast beneath the sweater, she shivered violently in a fierce rush of pleasure. At that moment she wanted only to belong to him—nothing else seemed to matter.

Bay's lips burned their way down her throat as he muttered hoarsely, "God, but I want you, Dany! I've needed this since the first moment I saw you."

Only dimly hearing his words, Dany locked her fingers in his hair to pull his lips back to hers. With an abandon that would later surprise her she fumbled with the buttons of his shirt, desperate to tear down every barrier keeping them apart. Heated flesh met in searing contact as he pushed up her sweater, and their lips fused together in mindless need.

The shrill demand of the telephone brought Dany's mind jarringly back to life. She stiffened in Bay's arms, tearing her lips from his as she began to struggle. "Let me go!"

Apparently believing that her sudden resistance was due to the phone rather than to her realization of what had nearly happened, Bay made no move to release her. "Let it ring," he ordered hoarsely.

"No—no, I have to answer it!" She pushed at his broad shoulders, turning her face away to avoid his seeking lips. "Let me go!"

With an impatient groan Bay rolled aside, allowing her to scramble hastily to her feet. She pulled her sweater into place and went over to the phone, picking up the receiver with a hand that trembled uncontrollably.

"Hello?"

"Dany, is that you? You don't sound like yourself."

She took a deep breath. "Oh . . . I'm fine, Jason. I had to rush to answer the phone, that's all." She heard a savage curse from behind her and had to force herself to concentrate on what Jason was saying.

"Honey, you promised to send me the outline for your next book. Where is it? When you were here, you said that you only had a couple more chapters to work out."

Dany was nervously aware of Bay's brooding presence just behind her, knowing that he was listening to her part of the conversation. She couldn't talk about the book! Her voice was strained when she said, "It isn't finished, Jason. I—I need more time."

"How much more time?"

"I—I don't know. Can I call you back tomorrow?"

There was a moment of silence, and then Jason said curiously, "I get the feeling that I interrupted something."

Dany released a laugh that sounded unnatural even to her own ears. "No, of course not, Jason. You didn't interrupt anything." A harsh laugh from Bay caused her fingers to tighten around the receiver.

Jason heard the laugh. His voice came gently over the line. "I don't want to pry, honey, but if you have a problem . . ."

Grateful tears rose in her eyes at his concern. "I'll be fine, Jason—really. And I'll call you tomorrow."

"Take care of yourself, Dany."

"I will. Bye, Jason." She cradled the receiver and turned to face Bay. He had refastened his shirt and was on his feet, and Dany's eyes widened at the glittering fury in his. They were a brilliant cobalt, flashing silvery sparks of rage.

"Can't Carrington leave you alone for two lousy weeks?" he demanded harshly. "Hell, Dany—he's more than twice your age!"

Dany blinked in confusion as she stared at him. "Jason is my friend, Bay. He—"

"Your friend! My God, but that's rich! Is he the reason you left New York in such a hurry? Did the two you have a little spat?"

"No. Bay, it's not what you're thinking. How many times do I have to tell you—"

"—that Carrington isn't your lover?" His voice was hard and cold. "And what about the conversation you just had with him? 'It isn't finished, Jason. I need more time'!" he mimicked cruelly. "Why do you need more time, Dany? So that you can decide whether or not to go back to him?"

Dany silently damned the rumors that had put such thoughts into his head. "Bay, please—"

He cut her off again. "You can't expect me to believe that the two of you aren't lovers now, Dany! Not now! Not after the way you responded to me!"

She stared at him, shocked to realize that he thought

her abandoned behavior had been the result of experience rather than desire for him alone. How could she explain that she had never felt such passion for any other man?

Her silence seemed to goad him further. "Oh, I have to hand it to you, Dany, you really had me fooled. I almost believed that there was nothing more than friendship between you and Carrington." His laugh was savage. "Is he the only one, or have there been others?"

A tiny flicker of hope rose in Dany's breast. "If I didn't know better, Bay . . . I'd think you were jealous."

His blue eyes fairly blazed with contempt. "You aren't worth jealousy, Dany! Mine, or any other man's!"

Hope died a bitter death. Bay would never learn to love her; he thought her a tramp. Trying to hold on to herself until he left, Dany turned away from him. "You'd better leave, Bay," she told him flatly.

"So Carrington's the lucky man, after all." His voice was strangely rough. "That's it, isn't it, Dany? You're going back to him."

"Good-bye, Bay." She wasn't about to let him see just how much his cruel words had hurt her.

"Not just yet." Hard fingers bit into her shoulders as he jerked her around to face him. "I want you, Dany, and I intend to take you—even if you do belong to Carrington!"

She barely had time to see that his face was gray and twisted with some emotion she had never seen before, and then his lips were crushing hers. There was no gentleness in his kiss: only driving need and black rage.

Frightened by the anger in him, and bitterly hurt by the things he had said, Dany found the strength to fight him. She tore her lips from his, straining every muscle to escape him. "No! Don't do this, Bay!" She might just as well have thrown her slight weight against a stone wall.

"Leave Carrington, Dany," he muttered hoarsely against her throat. "Come to me—I'll take care of you."

71

The man she loved wanted to make her his mistress; it was too much. Suddenly going limp in his arms, Dany covered her face with trembling hands and burst into tears.

Bay uttered a grating curse and released her, turning his back to her as she stumbled to a chair and sank down. "Tears!" he said bitterly. "A woman's most powerful weapon!"

Dany fought to control herself, but sobs shook her slender body for some time. She finally raised her head to stare at him through hurt tear-drenched eyes. "Damn you," she said in a low, shaking voice. "You're just like all the rest!"

He swung around to face her, but she gave him no opportunity to speak.

"You think that a woman can be bought or sold! Well, not this one! I don't belong to Jason or you or any other man! I belong to myself—and I'm not for sale!"

It might have been the raw hurt he saw in her eyes that caused his hard face to soften, or it might have been the knowledge that his behavior had been very much at fault. "I'm sorry, Dany. I lost my temper."

"Get out of here."

"Dany—"

"I said, get out!" She jumped to her feet. "Leave! Get out of my house and out of my life!"

He stared at her grimly. "It isn't over between us, Dany."

"Us?" She laughed bitterly. "There was never any 'us' It was all part of your campaign. I should have recognized the lines."

"It wasn't like that!"

"If you don't get out, I swear I'll call the police!" Her voice was very near the breaking point.

He hesitated and then swore beneath his breath. Turning on his heel, he left the house, closing the patio door with a force that should have shattered the glass.

Dany sank down in the chair, trying vainly to choke back her tears. It was over. A gruff bark from outside caused her to rise automatically and go over to open the door and let Brutus in. The huge animal seemed to sense that something was wrong, following her back to the chair and resting his head in her lap when she sat down.

Dany stroked the heavy head with trembling fingers. "If he comes back over here, bite him!" she ordered, her voice a forlorn thread of sound. "You hear me? Bite him!"

Brutus waved his long tail uncertainly, and Dany felt a half-hysterical laugh try to escape from her throat. She knew very well that the big dog would do no such thing. Bay seemed to have a knack with animals; he had won Brutus over as easily as he had won her over. Too easily. Too easily. . . .

She told herself to forget him. She told herself that she would one day find a man worthy of her love, a man who would *know* that she wasn't that kind of woman. She told herself that it would be an easy thing to dislodge Bay from her heart. She told herself every sane, logical thing she could think of. It didn't help. Bay had slipped beneath her guard, and she knew now that it had been deliberate. He had behaved so drastically unlike the rumors she had heard, she had begun to believe that those rumors were as false as the ones about herself.

Dany knew what he wanted, of course. He wanted her . . . and not only for his film. Wealthy, powerful, ruggedly handsome, he was obviously accustomed to getting what he wanted with scarcely a struggle, whether it be an actress for one of his films or a woman to warm his bed. God knew she had been warned. How many times had she heard tales of his ruthlessness, his determination? And she had believed those tales.

Until . . .

Until he had come to see her. Those cold, intelligent eyes had seen immediately that she disliked him, and he had been quick to develop tactics expressly designed to undermine that dislike. He had been friendly and charming, offering her a casual, undemanding friendship with no strings and no promises. She had been lulled into a mistaken sense of security, her guard dropping bit by bit, feeling herself safe and unthreatened in his company.

Looking back, Dany could recall several occasions when she had come upon a peculiar, watchful expression on his hard face. Watchful, brooding, waiting—like a cat at a mousehole, she had thought then, tensing himself for the killing pounce. And tonight he had pounced.

God, what a fool she had been! Blind, stupid, walking into his trap with all the unguarded innocence of a trusting child. She had made it easy for him! He had pulled on a mask every bit as deceptive as the one she had worn for years, and she had fallen for it—hook, line, and sinker. She never saw the bars of the trap closing on her until Jason's phone call had brought Bay's true opinion of her to light.

And thank God for Jason! If he had not called when he did, Dany knew very well that her treacherous body would have surrendered completely to Bay's demands. She had not known then that his only desire was to possess her body. She had been giving of herself completely, with her heart as well as her body, but Bay had been intent only on making another conquest. The realization sickened her. She had long ago vowed that she would never be just another notch on a man's belt, and if Jason had not called, that's just what she would have been.

Bitterness rushed through her body with the devastation of a forest fire, searing the bloom of her newly discovered love until it crumbled into ashes, leaving only the roots to be enveloped by a numbing cold. She was still sitting there, her eyes fixed on something only she could see, when the phone rang an hour later. Giving Brutus an abstracted pat, she rose and crossed to the phone. "Hello?"

"Dany?" It was Adam, his voice uncertain. "Sweetie, I know you said you didn't want to be bothered, but there's something I need to talk to you about."

"It's all right, Adam," she murmured absently. "I wasn't doing anything special. What is it?"

Relieved to have apparently caught her in a good mood, Adam's voice became brisk. "I have an assignment for you; it'll only take a couple of weeks, so you won't miss much of your vacation."

"Adam—"

"Hear me out, Dany, please. You've heard of Bud Carson, haven't you?"

Only mildly interested, Dany said, "He's some sort of patron of the arts. Throws huge parties for show people and artists. Jet-set type."

"Right. Well, he's become the patron of an up-and-coming young designer. The guy's good, Dany; I've seen some of his work. Carson wants to launch him this fall—and I do mean launch! Worldwide coverage. Anyway, he wants to have some of the more influential people in advertising stay at his lodge up in Connecticut. It's a rustic sort of place, stone fireplaces and weathered timbers—the kind of place you'd expect to meet a bear face-to-face on a morning stroll."

Dany smiled slightly, accurately reading the note of faint distaste in her employer's voice. Adam was city born-and-bred, and had never been able to understand the desire of some of his fellow men to go off into the wilderness in order to recharge their souls. "Adam, I really don't see—"

75

"Hang on, I'm coming to it. Carson wants these advertisers to meet the designer and see some of his creations. And those creations will look a damn sight better if a beautiful model happens to be wearing them."

"I'm on vacation."

"Well, that's what I told him." Adam sounded harassed. "This thing came right out of the blue, Dany; Carson only called me a few minutes ago. He wants everything settled tonight and he says he won't take no for an answer."

That remark set up a train of thought that was unexpectedly painful. Dany pushed it away and wondered miserably why everything she heard seemed to bring Bay to her mind.

"Come on, angel," Adam said persuasively. "It's only two weeks! All you have to do is parade around in pretty dresses and pose for a few pictures. You don't have to worry about any propositions, because Carson's happily married and always adopts a fatherly attitude to lovely girls. He'll make sure that none of his guests bothers you too. You'll love the place. There are horses and mountain trails, and whenever you aren't needed, you can wander around all you want."

Listening to him in silence, Dany suddenly realized that she wanted very much to get away from the beach. If she stayed here, she would have too much time to think, and that wasn't what she needed right now. At least at this lodge, she would probably be fairly busy and surrounded by people. A sneering little voice in her head told her that she was simply running away on the slim chance that Bay might come back and try his luck again, but she ignored it.

Sensing that she was wavering in her determination to accept no more assignments until the fall, Adam's voice became even more persuasive. "You'll enjoy yourself, sweetie, I promise you! Most of the guests you already know. In fact, I believe that Jason will be there."

Surprised, Dany said, "But Jason isn't in advertising! It's one of the few things he *isn't* into."

Rather dryly, Adam responded, "He's an important man in New York, Dany, and you know it. If he takes a shine to this designer, he could easily help smooth the way for him."

"I suppose." Dany sighed. "Adam, I really don't think —"

"As a favor to me, Dany?" His voice suddenly dropped sheepishly. "I don't like the idea of offending him. Besides, the offer he made was very respectable." He hesitated for a moment, then said suddenly, "Respectable, *hell*—it was staggering. Took my breath away. Don't say no, Dany."

"Well," she hedged, "will there be other models?"

"Susan and"—he hesitated slightly—"Marissa."

Dany had worked with them both. Susan was a bubbly girl of Dany's own age, brunet and dark-eyed, with a warm heart and a friendly smile. Like Dany, she was waiting only until her contract was up before giving up modeling. She, however, was giving it up to marry the man she loved, a photographer.

Marissa, on the other hand . . . How could one sum up Marissa? She had the cool, Nordic beauty that usually accompanied blond hair and blue eyes, her features as classically perfect as those of a Greek statue. But the perfection of her face was lessened by the hard glint of avariciousness in her eyes. Her fingernails were always long and polished bright red. They were like the painted claws of a predatory cat, but they were not her weapons. Dany had seen her shatter younger models at ten paces with three sweetly uttered words.

She herself had never been particularly vulnerable to Marissa's acid tongue. She was aware that the older woman hated her bitterly and resented her swift and relatively easy rise to fame. The higher Dany's star climbed, the more malicious the sweet voice had become. But Dany, shielded by her aloof mask—and not driven by Marissa's fiercely competitive nature—found it easy to ignore the poisonous darts. She had been amused rather than angry to watch the blonde demand, as her right, the attention of every man within sight. And woe to any man who made the error of showing an interest in Dany when Marissa was around. In no time flat he would find himself caught in the coils of the blonde's seductive beauty. But then, having drawn blood, she would stroll away like a satisfied feline, content at having—at least in her own mind—stolen Dany's admirer from her. With her long fingers flexing in an unconsciously grasping gesture, she would fix her eyes on still another quarry, paying no attention to the poor landed fish who gasped for air in her wake. The road behind her was strewn with her victims.

Not that Marissa had always come out on top. She had tried her tricks once too often, and that was why Dany was hesitating now. Just over a year before, Marissa had tried to get her claws into Bay Spencer. Dany had not been present, of course, but Susan had told her later what had happened. It appeared that Bay had been the one to draw blood, turning away from the blonde with yawning boredom, and leaving her to rage impotently over her inability to ensnare him as she had so many others.

Cynically Dany wondered if Bay had realized how very alike he and Marissa were. Was that why he had turned away from her—because he had not been able to stomach a female version of himself? She thought not; Bay would not have been able to see his own faults with such clarity.

Dany shook the thoughts away and tried to make up her mind about this assignment. If it were not for Marissa's presence, she would not hesitate, but Dany wasn't completely certain that she would be indifferent, this time, to the older woman's insults. Still quivering beneath the crushing weight of a bitter one-sided love, she knew herself to be vulnerable to shafts that had glanced off her armor only months before.

Of course, if Marissa knew what had happened between the man she still craved and the woman she hated, she would do everything in her power to tear Dany to pieces, but Dany comforted herself with the thought that she could not possibly know. There would only be the same old insults—and surely she could deal with those, couldn't she?

Realizing that she had been silent for some time, she finally spoke to the patiently waiting Adam. "Does it have to be Marissa?" she asked rather dryly.

"With the size of the fee offered?" Adam laughed sardonically. "She snapped it up! Sorry, Dany; she was standing right here when the call came. I was working late here in the office, and she stopped by on the way to some party or other to ask about a new assignment. That woman's like a steamroller; I never had a chance." He sighed. "Carson asked for a blonde, a brunette, and a redhead. He specified you as the redhead. As a matter of fact, he said that if you wouldn't do it, the whole deal was off."

"I'll bet Marissa liked hearing that," Dany murmured, smiling in spite of herself.

"Credit me with a little common sense," Adam requested wryly. "I made damn sure she knows nothing about that particular part of the conversation." He paused for a moment then said in a cajoling voice, "What do you say, sweetie? You're tough enough to take on Marissa—in fact, I've often thought that you could make mincemeat of her if you wanted to—and none of the rest will bother you."

Slowly Dany asked, "Who's the photographer?"

Cheerfully Adam said, "Cy Bennet. You won't have to worry about friendly hands on this assignment."

That, Dany knew, was true. Cy was Susan's fiancé and had eyes for no one else. She hesitated for a moment and then sighed ruefully. "Okay, Adam, I'll go. The beach has pretty much lost its appeal for me anyway."

The faintly forlorn note escaped Adam. "Terrific. You can fly out anytime, Dany. Just cable Carson and let him know what flight you'll be on; he'll meet you at the airport. He said to tell you that the guests will start arriving Monday, but the designer is already there, so the sooner you arrive, the better." He hesitated. "As a matter of fact, I've reserved space—tentatively, that is!" he added hastily— "on the midnight flight from Portland to Hartford. Uh—if that's all right, of course."

Dany glanced at the clock and sighed. "You're not giving me much time, Adam. Packing, driving to Portland, taking Brutus to the kennel . . ."

"I'm not giving you the chance to back out," he told her frankly. "You just get ready and take off, sweetie. I'll confirm the seat and let Carson know."

"But I'll arrive there in the middle of the night," Dany protested, offering a last objection.

"More like dawn," he said calmly. "It's not a direct flight. But don't worry about it; Carson said he'd meet you no matter what time it was, so I took him at his word."

"If looks could travel through telephone lines like words can . . ." she began threateningly.

"I know," he soothed. "I'd be cut to ribbons. Tell me all about it—as soon as you finish this assignment!"

Mentally throwing her hands up in defeat, Dany said, "I'll look forward to it!" and hung up rather abruptly on Adam's quiet laugh.

CHAPTER FIVE

A quick call to the kennel to warn of Brutus's arrival, and then Dany was packing hastily, throwing clothing into cases that had been empty for barely two weeks. Thoughts of Bay hovered at the back of her mind like the nagging ache of an unexplored pain, but she managed to keep them just out of reach of conscious thought. In an effort to keep the hurting thoughts at a distance, she wondered idly why she had never succumbed to Adam's considerable charms.

He was slightly above medium height and fair, his blond hair falling over his brow in a boyish manner, his smile a flash of white teeth. He was probably, she thought, nearly as ruthless as Bay in some ways, but his determination was never obvious, and he knew when and how to bow out gracefully from a situation. He had remained single for nearly thirty-five years, and had long been called one of the most eligible bachelors in New York. His success he owed to his charming manner and an infallible instinct for market trends.

He had never got involved with any of his models, having the sense to keep business and pleasure carefully separated. When Jason had introduced him to Dany, he had first seen her only as a potentially great model, and his first act had been to get her name on a contract. She had spent those first few weeks around the studio, and Adam had started coming into the room where she was being photographed by various artists, telling them exactly what he wanted for Dany's portfolio. By the time the portfolio had been completed, he had broken his own rule and asked Dany out. She had refused.

Still torn over the deaths of her parents and bewildered by the strange new world she had been thrust into, Dany shied nervously away from any sort of a relationship. She had no idea of the power her beauty gave her; the looks of men who watched her—their eyes flickering with desire—had sent her scurrying into a shell.

Adam had been unable to break through that shell, though he had often tried during that first year. After that, he had finally given up. Their relationship had always been that of employer and employee, nothing more. He had grown to know her though, over the years. He knew that she flatly refused to work with photographers known for their wandering hands; that she hated parties and was strangely terrified of reporters; that she was completely unconscious of her own beauty and baffled by men's reaction to it.

Dany had never considered him a friend, but she knew that if she were ever in trouble, she could turn to him and he would help in any way he could. What he thought of her supposed relationship with Jason only he knew, but he had never shown her a lack of respect, and she was grateful to him for that. And that was it. She had never felt the smallest interest in Adam as a man, and that, along with disgruntled comments from men who had made no headway with her, had made her wonder if perhaps she was frigid.

She knew now that that was not the case. Bay had proved that much. And a part of her wanted to curse him bitterly for it. Until he had come along, she had been more or less content in her life. Her body had remained unawakened until he had touched it; her heart had remained whole and her own—not torn from her breast by a man who had no use for it. Perhaps she *had* been existing in the shadows, but at least there was no pain there. Bay had torn her from that peaceful haven, and he had done so with the worst of intentions. He had believed the hateful rumors about her, and that was the most ironic thing of all. If only she had believed the rumors about *him*!

Dany straightened abruptly, her features tightening in pain as she realized where her unwary thoughts had led. Her newly awakened senses were clamoring for satisfaction, as they had from the moment she had pulled herself from Bay's arms. Thrusting the realization away, she quickly changed into slacks and a blouse. Picking up her suitcase and the smaller vanity case, she went quickly from the bedroom. She was suddenly very eager to leave this house, and she hoped desperately that she could also leave her memories here as well.

She loaded the cases into her small rental car, saw Brutus safely installed in the backseat, and began the long drive to Portland. Since she had never been fond of driving at night, all her attention was focused on the darkened highway, and she was able to push everything else from her mind. Once in Portland, she took a reluctant Brutus to his kennel, hastily turned her car in at the airport, and barely managed to make her flight.

The events of the day had exhausted her, and once the plane was safely in the air, she pushed back her seat, ignoring the interested glances of the young man on the aisle, and tried to sleep. She had no hope of actually being able to rest, but nature has its own healing devices, and sleep was one of them. The emotions of the day had taken their toll, and her mind curtained itself in darkness.

She did not awaken when the plane landed at some darkened point midway across the country, and since her seat belt was still fastened, the stewardess made no effort to rouse her. She did not have to change planes, and the activities of those who did failed to disturb her. The disappointed young man on the aisle was replaced by a keen-eyed older man, and Dany still did not stir. The plane took off again, proceeding on its way to Hartford. Dany slept on.

She woke with a start when a hand touched her shoulder and she looked up into the apologetic eyes of the stewardess. "I'm sorry, Miss Morgan, but we're about to serve breakfast, and I wasn't sure if you wanted to miss it."

Dany hastily put up a hand to smother a yawn and smiled slightly. "It's all right. I needed the sleep, but I also need the food. Thank you."

The young woman smiled and nodded. "I'll be bringing it along in a minute. We'll touch down in Hartford in about an hour."

Her green eyes drowsy, Dany nodded and watched the stewardess make her way along the narrow aisle. It was then that she became aware of the fixed stare of the man on the aisle. He looked to be in his late thirties or early forties, distinguished in a dark, well-cut business suit; his rugged face could by no stretch of the imagination be considered handsome. He was, in fact, almost ugly, but that impression was swiftly belied by the strange beauty of his long-lashed violet eyes.

When Dany turned fully to face him, he gave a slight start and murmured, "God bless my soul! You're Danica Morgan! I didn't think I was mistaken after the stewardess spoke your name."

Her mind still half-shrouded in the mists of sleep, Dany gave him the polite smile she reserved for those occasions when someone recognized her and wondered rather absently if she could bear to eat anything.

"You're the image of your mother, child."

It was like a cool breeze blowing the cobwebs from her brain. She stared at the man, her attention fully caught. "I—did you know my mother?"

He smiled slightly. "Long before you were born." The beautiful violet eyes grew misty with memories, the smile sweeping the last vestige of ugliness from his face. "She was a lovely little thing, Katie was. Sweet and gentle—with an Irish temper that couldn't be bested."

Dany laughed in spite of herself. "You seem to have known her well. But you don't look old enough—"

He chuckled as she broke off in dismay. "Bless you, child. I'm forty-six."

Relieved that he had not been offended, Dany smiled in return. "Well, I'm twenty-five—hardly a child."

His rich chuckle broke from him again. "Don't remind me, child. I'd hate for it to happen again!" The violet eyes went over her in a single comprehensive sweep, and the twinkle in them deepened. "If it did, I bloody well *know* I'd go off and shoot myself!"

Dany was torn between amusement at the frank appreciation in his eyes and confusion at his words. "I'm afraid I don't understand."

"If things had been different, I might have been your father." He nodded as her eyes widened slightly. "That's it. I lost out to Daniel. He showed up with that bloody absentminded smile of his, and your mother went down for the count." There was no bitterness in his deep voice, only a sort of rueful amusement. "I could have cheerfully drowned myself and nearly did when Daniel asked me to be his best man. If I'd had any sense, I would have drowned *him*, except that I knew your mother would never forgive me. So I was Daniel's best man and even managed to toast the bride and groom after the ceremony —God knows how." His smile was reminiscent. "He was quite a man, your father. Classy."

Her more bitter recent memories forgotten for the moment, Dany smiled at him, happy to have discovered someone who had known her beloved parents. He gave a slight start, and said wryly, "Lord, child, I've forgotten my manners! My name's Tremaine—Darius Tremaine."

It was Dany's turn to start. "Of course! Darius. My mother mentioned you many times—and so did Daddy."

Darius looked surprised and not a little moved. "Did they now," he murmured. "I would have expected them to forget all about me."

Dany laughed softly. "Mama always said that you had the most beautiful smile in the world—except for Daddy's."

That beautiful smile swept across his face again, along with a slight flush. The arrival of the stewardess with their breakfast gave him time to compose himself, and when she had left their trays, he cast a sidelong teasing glance at Dany's face. "The *image* of your mother," he said definitely.

Dany laughed and they began to talk casually as they ate. Darius told her about his somewhat footloose life of the past twenty-five years, describing his wanderings with the skill of a natural-born storyteller. From his talk she gathered that he was wealthy, since he spoke of a penthouse apartment in New York and a cattle ranch in Texas —and she knew damn well that neither of those came cheaply. He had apparently amassed most of his money himself, speculating in various ventures, and pulling out of them when they became losing propositions or when the restless urge to move on overcame him. He seemed to have no ties, mentioned no family, and Dany wondered a little sadly if he had ever really got over his lovely Katie.

She forgot her own troubles, listening to him talk with real interest, and it was not until the stewardess removed their trays that the pain of yesterday was recalled. Darius was the unwitting cause of it. He sat back as the trays were taken away, surveying her with a teasing smile. "That's enough about me. What about you? I know how your career's going, but what of the rest of your life? A lovely young woman like you is bound to have men chasing her wherever she goes. Is there a special one yet?"

His smile faded as he watched the light in her fine eyes snuffed out like a candle's flame, the delicate bones of her face seeming to clench in on themselves as though she were in the grip of some terrible pain. And then she was smiling again, her face only a little strained, and her eyes slightly guarded.

"Not yet," she replied lightly. "I'll probably end up being an old maid."

He turned slightly in his seat in order to better study her face, his own very somber. After a moment, he said in a soft, gruff voice, "I'm sorry, child. It happens that way sometimes. To the best of us . . . and the worst of us."

Dany felt her throat tighten suddenly, realizing that her helpless reaction to Bay's memory had given her away. She looked at him, seeing the gentle expression in his strange eyes, and she wanted to tell him the whole story. She wanted to cast herself on his broad chest and sob out her pain and bitterness. Only one thing stiffened her spine and brought a faint light of courage into her eyes, and that was the inescapable knowledge that he would be second best to her—just as he had been to her mother. It was Bay's shoulder she wanted to cry on, his metallic cobalt eyes she wanted to gaze at her with gentleness, and no matter how bitter that knowledge was, she accepted it as truth.

Her instinct told her that Darius was oddly vulnerable where she was concerned, because she was the image of the woman he had loved, and because she herself was vulnerable. His earlier words about shooting himself had not been entirely in jest, she knew. He could love her very easily, seeing her in his mind as a recreation of her mother, and she could quite easily grow to love him because his gentleness would spread a soothing balm over her wounded, aching heart.

Dany was inwardly amazed at the clarity of her perception, the certainty of her thoughts. Bay had done this to her. He had left her emotions raw, but he had also opened her eyes to herself and to those around her. The gauzy curtain that she had hung between herself and the world was gone, and she knew that she would never be indifferent to emotion again. She would laugh and cry—and bleed just like the rest of the human race. She would feel everything with all the depth she was capable of. And somewhere, deep inside herself, unacknowledged by her conscious mind, a tiny seed of gratitude toward Bay was planted.

Unaware that he was still watching her intently, unaware that the shutters had gone from her eyes and that the shimmering green depths were clearly showing everything as one emotion swiftly suceeded another, Dany stared at Darius without seeing him, her mind caught up in this strange new discovery of herself.

As for the man seated at her side, he was watching her and slowly beginning to acknowledge to himself that this lovely young woman was not the girl he had loved so long ago, any more than he was the young man who had loved so fiercely. Silently, for the first time, he said a gentle good-bye to the woman who, in his eyes, had died twenty-six years ago, and who had died in reality five years ago. The memory of her, of them, was tucked away with tender finality in a sunlit corner of his mind and heart, with no power to hurt him any longer.

Strangely, both of them came back to the present at the same moment, releasing twin sighs of burdens lifted—and of burdens accepted. Dany, blinking, found that he was watching her still, but with a different expression in his violet eyes. It was a calm, paternal light that could appreciate her beauty and youth without yearning for it; sympathize with her ill-fated love without wishing to take advantage of it. She realized then that they had both, in separate ways, come to the same conclusions about themselves and each other. They were separated by a gulf of experience that neither wished to cross, and both were content with that.

Dany smiled slightly. "Yesterday was . . . not a good day. I'm afraid I haven't quite recovered yet."

"You will." His voice was quiet and very firm. "You may not believe that now, but one day you'll look back and find that yesterday is only a memory."

The pilot advised them to fasten their seat belts at that moment, and Dany only nodded. She watched Darius comply with the request, her hand moving automatically to check the fastening of her own belt. As the plane banked slightly she looked over at him and said casually, "I've never been to Hartford. Are you staying there?"

He turned his head to smile at her. "Not in Hartford, no. A friend of mine has a lodge about forty miles outside the city. He has some young designer under his wing and wants me to help sponsor the boy."

Startled, she asked, "You mean, Bud Carson?"

One of Darius's dark eyebrows shot up. "Know him?"

"Not yet." Dany started to laugh. "That's where I'm going now—I'm going to model the designer's creations."

A pleased expression spread across his deeply tanned face. "Well, now—that's what I call good news! I was imagining I'd be bored stiff at Bud's, but now I see that I'll enjoy myself after all. He called me a couple of days ago with the invitation, but he didn't mention any models."

"Apparently he just made up his mind to have models last night," Dany told him with a slight grimace. "My boss called and told me about it, and since I was—getting a little tired of my own company, I decided to take the assignment."

Darius nodded. "Good. You and I can get to know each other in the next couple of weeks. That is—you are staying that long, aren't you?"

"Adam—my boss—said that the assignment would take about two weeks, so I assume I'll be staying at least that long. It all depends on Carson, I guess."

With a chuckle Darius said, "I'll see if I can persuade him to invite you to stay on after this gathering of his is over."

Dany smiled at him, suddenly feeling much more cheerful about the future. She honestly didn't think that she would ever get over Bay completely, but the only thing she felt for him at the moment was bitterness, and something bordering closely on hatred, and those were certainly much less painful than the agony she had felt after hearing exactly what he thought of her.

She and Darius talked together idly while the plane landed and wandered about on the tarmac until it had found its own particular niche. When the pilot was finally satisfied with the position of his plane, the passengers were told, in the manner of an adult speaking to helpless children, that they could deplane now, and Dany and her companion joined the throng of weary passengers approaching the exit. Darius was familiar with the airport, and in no time at all they had collected their luggage and were stepping out into the chill dawn air.

A sleek black limousine was drawn up among the rank of cabs, and as Darius led Dany forward, a dignified-looking chauffeur got out of the car and came to meet them. "Miss Morgan, Mr. Tremaine." He did not appear surprised to see the two of them together. "Mr. Carson offers his apologies for not being here to meet you; he is expecting a transatlantic phone call and was forced to remain at the lodge."

Darius nodded easily at the middle-aged man. "That's quite all right, Frazier." The chauffeur took the two cases from Darius and locked them away in the trunk, while Darius helped Dany into the backseat of the car. Within moments the car was threading its way through Hartford's early-morning traffic.

Dany glanced at the glass separating them from the driver and then looked at Darius. "I wonder how the chauffeur—Frazier?—knew who I was."

"That's easy." Darius smiled at her. "Bud probably told him to look for a gorgeous redhead!" He studied her slightly pale face for a moment then said, "When we reach the lodge, I think you'd better try to get a little sleep. You look beat."

Dany set her vanity case down at her feet, and gave him a slightly weary smile. "I thought the nap on the plane would help, but I feel as though I could sleep for a week."

"Well, the rest of the crowd won't start arriving until Monday, so you'll have a chance to catch up on your rest. Bud's a lazy host. You'll find out that he leaves his guests pretty much to themselves."

Dany was aware that there were many questions she wanted to ask her new friend, but she was just too tired to think at the moment. She had not felt particularly tired on the plane, but once on her feet, she had been almost overcome by sheer physical exhaustion. She did not think of Bay. Instead, she stared out the window of the car, the dawn light granting her only a glimpse of the sprawling city they soon left behind.

Slightly more than an hour later, the car turned off a somewhat lonely highway and onto an even more deserted blacktop road. At first Dany assumed that it was a public road, but she soon realized that it was, in fact, a private drive. It wandered among gently rolling hills thickly planted with maples and evergreens; spring flowers of every type burst forth in a blaze of color among the bright green of the grass.

The car rounded a bend five minutes after turning off the highway, and the lodge came into view. Dany's vague mental picture of the place had not prepared her for the sheer size of Carson's "retreat," and she was taken aback to realize that it could easily house a normal-size convention. Nestling in a valley between three thickly wooded hills, the lodge was built almost entirely of native stone and wood. The central portion was a tremendous A-frame, the crest of which must have been at least thirty feet from the ground. Huge panes of tinted glass fronted the structure, glittering in the morning sunlight. On each side of the central A-frame, the lodge spread out and (Dany was to find later) back, so that from above it would present the appearance of a box with one side missing. As he helped her from the car Darius told her that the lodge virtually surrounded a large and beautiful garden that Carson took a justifiable pride in.

Leaving the chauffeur to deal with their luggage, Darius led Dany up the stone steps to a set of double doors fashioned of heavy oak and decorated with gleaming brass handles. Before they could reach the doors, they were flung open in welcome, and a heavyset middle-aged man with graying hair and shrewd gray eyes came out to meet them. "Darius! Good to see you, man, good to see you! Glad you could make it!"

Darius shook hands with his host, a faint twinkle in his violet eyes, then gestured to Dany. "Bud, this is Miss Morgan."

Dany's hand was immediately lost in Carson's friendly clasp. "Miss Morgan! I'd recognize you anywhere, my dear; you're as lovely as your pictures."

"Please—call me Dany." She smiled rather tiredly at him, grateful for the welcome.

"Dany it is, then. And my friends call me Bud." Taking the arms of his guests, he led them through the opened doors and into the lodge.

Blinking slightly, Dany realized that the central A-frame was one large room, with archways on either wall giving access to the rest of the building. Two steps, almost immediately in front of the double doors, led down into the sunken great room. Deep brown carpet covered the floor; the walls were paneled in rich oak. The northern wall of the huge room was covered almost entirely in bookcases that were laden with trophies and plaques as well as books. The focal point of the room, however, was the tremendous stone fireplace gracing the far wall, and stretching all the way up to the point of the heavily beamed ceiling.

Before Dany could do more than notice that the room was furnished with innumerable chairs and sofas made of leather and some heavy material she could not identify, her host had claimed her attention.

"The kitchen, dining room, study, and game room are all on that side," he told her, gesturing toward the archway on the left of the great room. "The bedrooms are all on the other side." He shot a perceptive look at her pale face and said, "I'll show you to your bedrooms now, and *you,* young lady, had better get some rest. You sleep as long as you like; no one will disturb you."

Dany smiled faintly at the fatherly command, wondering rather dryly how many pseudofathers a girl could accumulate in a lifetime. She and Darius followed their host through the archway on the right and down a carpeted hallway. Dany lost track of the number of doors they passed, but she found that her bedroom was the first door past the turn in the hall. The chauffeur carried her suitcase in as she was standing by the door, and she promised Bud that she would rest, before smiling at Darius and quietly closing the door.

Her bedroom was decorated in shades of green and gold, with a matching adjoining bath, and Dany spared little more than a glance for it before locating a nightgown in her case, swiftly changing into it, and sliding between the cool sheets of the large comfortable bed. She was dead tired, and she fully intended to sleep as long as she could.

When she finally awoke, she was surprised to find that it was only a little after noon. After checking her watch, which she had reset at the airport, she tried to go back to sleep but found it impossible. With a faint grimace she finally threw back the covers and climbed out of the bed. It took only a few minutes to unpack and put her clothes away, and then she took a quick shower and dressed in white jeans and a green pullover top. Slipping her feet into a pair of sandals, she left her room and headed for the kitchen, her stomach having apparently forgotten its early breakfast.

During the next two days, she found that Darius had been right about their host: Carson left them more or less to themselves. His wife was visiting family out West, and except for the housekeeper Dany found that she was the only woman at the lodge. It didn't bother her, because both Darius and Bud seemed to see her as a temporarily adopted daughter. As for the young designer—whom she had met over lunch the first day—he was no problem at all.

Tony Blake was a slender young man with huge, soulful dark eyes and overlong black hair that flopped continually over his forehead. He was the sort of man who somehow managed to awake maternal instincts in most women. When they had first been introduced, Dany had seen a glint of appreciation in his black eyes, but she knew very well that that was due more to his profession than to his sex; in his mind, Dany was simply a form over which he draped his magnificent creations. His talk was full of materials and colors, fads and fashions, and after seeing some of his designs, Dany had to admit that Carson had made a wise decision in choosing to sponsor him.

Dany spent many hours wandering in Bud's lovely garden, finding a calm there that she could not find inside her own mind. The clarity of mind that she had discovered on the plane was still with her, but that did not seem to help when her thoughts were focused on the man she loved. And she did still love him. It was a bitter, hurting love, something that had been beautiful and was now twisted and thorny, but it was still love. She wanted to hurt him as he had hurt her, to punish him for his contempt. For the first time in her life she felt the desire to destroy another human being—and that knowledge sickened her.

Her treacherous mind kept calling forth memories of a charming, teasing companion with intelligence and a sense of humor; she felt herself reliving those first two weeks with an intensity that frightened her. She could remember every word, every gesture, every flash of his blue eyes. The restlessness of her body—awakened and yet unfulfilled, burning for some satisfaction beyond her knowledge—

disturbed her. It was as if Bay had lighted a fuse deep inside her and left it burning toward an unknown end.

She had never been so confused in her life. Bay's suddenly unveiled contempt for her, his belief in the rumors about her, had left a bitter wound, but what really hurt was the knowledge that she had been betrayed. *Betrayed.* Her untouched heart had reached out trustingly to him, believing that she had found a kindred spirit, only to discover that she had been nothing more than a body he wanted to possess.

That was why her love was tangled up with hatred. That was why she felt this terrible desire for revenge. He had rejected her love without even recognizing it for what it was, seeing her response to him only as that of an experienced woman in the arms of an equally experienced man. If Jason had not called when he had, Dany knew that she would have ended up with an even deeper wound, because she would have given herself to him body and soul.

Wandering among roses, and hedges sculpted in the shapes of various animals, Dany thought to herself that at least she had been spared the humiliation of seeing the triumph in his eyes. He could not have been sure that she had pulled herself from his arms only because of the phone; could not be certain that he had, in fact, made another conquest. It was a small sop, but it served to lessen the bitterness in her heart.

She watched the sun slide from sight behind the gently rolling hills surrounding the lodge, and thought with brief amusement that Adam's idea of mountains was not her own. He had been right about the horses—she had seen stables out behind the lodge, but had not yet found the desire to go for a ride—but as for mountain trails

. . . well, that was something else entirely. Thickly wooded trails, certainly, and possibly hilly ones, but the only mountains were the ones in Adam's mind.

With a faint sigh Dany turned toward the house. All the bedrooms had patio doors that opened onto the garden, and she chose to enter the house through her own room. The only thing Carson demanded of his guests was that they put in an appearance for before-dinner drinks, and since it was nearly that time, Dany decided to go straight to her room and change. She didn't feel very sociable, but she knew that the ritual would become more demanding as the lodge slowly filled with guests, and since the first of those were due to arrive the next day, she was ruefully grateful for the opportunity to practice her aloof mask.

The mask was more than a little cracked after its exposure to Bay's ruthless tactics, but it still existed, and Dany was determined that it would continue to do so. She had no intention of allowing anyone to see how badly she had been hurt. Her pride would not allow that.

She stepped into her bedroom and closed the glass door behind her, surprised to find a shimmering green dress laid out on her bed. It was emerald-green, the exact same shade as her eyes, and she remembered Tony showing it to her the day before. A folded piece of paper rested on top of the dress and, reading the note, Dany found that Tony wanted her to wear the dress tonight because some of the guests had already arrived. She wondered vaguely why he had left a note instead of coming in search of her, then decided that it was probably because he was busy with the early arrivals.

Half an hour later she was standing in front of the full-length mirror in her bathroom and staring, with some surprise, at her reflected image. The silky calf-length gown clung like a live thing to her slender figure, molding every curve with a loving hand. The design was an unusual one,

97

and it had taken Dany some time to figure out how it was supposed to be worn. Once on, the dress appeared to hold to her body with nothing more than sheer willpower. It had no sleeves, no back, and practically no front. As if by the wave of a magician's wand, the silky material gently cupped her full white breasts, leaving little to the imagination before sliding down smoothly to cover her waist and hips in a close-fitting sheath. A slit in the side left one shapely leg bare almost to the hip.

Dany drew a deep breath in appreciation of Tony's genius and made a startling discovery. Torn between horror and amusement, she made a mental note to breathe very carefully during the evening; anything else, and she looked as though she were about to come out of the damn thing! She spent several minutes walking around her bedroom, bending over, turning suddenly, until she was certain that the danger of imminent undress was only an illusion. But what a clever illusion! It was a gown expressly designed to catch and hold a man's attention, and Dany knew that she had never worn anything so blatantly seductive in her life.

Pausing before the mirror above her dresser, she made a final check to see that her hair remained in its braided coronet, suddenly conscious of a somewhat wistful desire that Bay should see her in this dress. Immediately she pushed the thought away, chiding herself mentally for such a stupid and completely useless desire. But she couldn't help thinking, as she headed toward the great room, that it probably wouldn't have made any difference if Bay *had* seen her this way. He would still have believed her to be a tramp—probably more so, she decided wryly. The thought stiffened her spine, and her aloof mask descended to veil her expression as she stepped through the archway and into the great room.

It was a spectacular entrance—all the more so because

the room was unexpectedly full of people and most of them were men. Dany made no attempt to call attention to herself; her innocently seductive beauty, intensified by the gown she wore, did that with no help at all from her.

Trying to ignore the tremor of panic in her stomach, Dany told herself sternly that *of course,* there weren't thirty people in the room—it just looked that way. She was fighting a craven desire to turn and run, painfully aware of the almost reverent silence in the room, when two men detached themselves from the cluster in front of the fireplace and came to greet her.

Tony was the first to reach her, his dark eyes sweeping her body in an entirely professional manner, but with a glint of purely masculine appreciation in their depths. "Dany, that gown is perfect for you," he told her in his soft, rapid way. "I thought at first that I had overestimated your bust size, but I see now that I was right, after all."

Five years in the modeling trade had taught Dany to take such frank comments without loss of composure, but she was aware of a flicker of gratitude that Tony's voice was too low to be heard by anyone but her. Keeping her own voice low, she asked wryly, "What did you have in mind when you designed this thing, Tony? I mean, am I supposed to lean against a lamppost, or what?"

He chuckled softly. "I designed it for you, to take advantage of your natural, God-given attributes—and if you don't know what they are, I won't bother telling you!"

Since conversation in the room had resumed Dany felt some of the tension leave her, and she was able to smile at the compliment. "Well, all I know is that I feel like I'll come out of this dress if I so much as twitch the wrong muscle!"

"You won't," he stated confidently.

Dany absently raised a hand to rub the back of her neck as she stared at him. "You know that," she said, her voice still low, "and I know that—but do the rest of these people know it?" The dress had already given her a pretty fair idea of how Tony's mind worked, so she was not much surprised to hear him reply in the tone of one who knew his fellow man well.

"Are you kidding? Every man in this room is now making a bet with himself as to when that dress decides to leave you."

"That being your intention, I suppose?"

"Sure. Men like looking at lovely women, and lovely women like being looked at." He winked at her and turned away, just as Darius came up.

With a gallant bow his violet eyes somehow managing to be grave and laughing at once, he handed her a drink and murmured, "That's quite a dress you almost have on. I'm sure the men in this room need a drink worse than you do, but Bud can't bear to see anyone with empty hands."

Smiling at the gently teasing voice, Dany murmured, "Believe me, I would not have chosen this thing on my own. You have to admit that Tony has talent though."

"He certainly does." Darius sipped his drink thoughtfully. "I can see now why Bud decided to sponsor him. By the way—just in passing—is it safe for you to wander around in that dress?"

"Perfectly safe. I think." She rubbed her neck again with her free hand, and then suddenly stiffened as awareness of her action burst in on her. Blank green eyes swung from her regard of Darius's face to search out the room.

He was leaning against the fireplace, a drink in his hand and cold, metallic eyes fixed on Dany. As her gaze was drawn to him like a moth to a destructive flame, Bay Spencer raised his glass in a mocking toast.

CHAPTER SIX

For all their coldness those eyes burned her, searing through the illusory promise of the silken gown and scorching the tender flesh beneath. They stole her breath, just as an actual physical caress would have done, stripping her bare of everything but the instinctively held mask. Shock held her rigid for a long moment, while the crucible of his eyes sent a treacherous weakness flowing through her limbs, a feverish heat forming in her loins.

With an effort that was actually painful she tore her gaze from his and hastily raised the drink to her lips, swallowing half of it in one gulp. Immediately the fiery spirit spread through her body, dispersing the shock and lending a bastard strength to her unsteady legs. Unaccustomed to alcohol, the fireball making its way toward her stomach succeeded in diverting her mind, at least temporarily, from the bewildering knowledge of Bay's presence. "What is this?" she asked Darius breathlessly.

"A daiquiri, heavy on the rum," Darius replied, his voice quivering with amusement. "Bud likes his guests to be happy."

"Happy or senseless?"

He chuckled, then reached out a hand hastily to stop her as she started to raise the glass to her lips again. "Careful, there! I don't think you're used to drinking, and that stuff can put you away."

With more than a suggestion of gritted teeth Dany ignored the warning and took another sip. "They say there's no time like the present," she said rather grimly, "and I think it's high time I learned to drink!"

Darius started to reply, and then stiffened suddenly, a frown crossing his dark face. With an odd gesture he shifted his weight slightly, the wide shoulders flexing as though to ward off an unfriendly hand. "Someone staring holes through me," he murmured, almost to himself. When Dany looked puzzled, he relaxed and smiled down at her. "An instinct I picked up in South America. I never knew who was waiting to stab me in the back," he explained. "After a while I developed an itch between my shoulder blades—sort of a private radar."

Dany, who knew the feeling well, tried to ignore a desire to look across the room at Bay and murmured, "I doubt that anyone here wants to stab you, Darius."

"One of your admirers, no doubt," he responded lightly.

"Dany—darling!"

With a start of surprise Dany turned to find Marissa bearing down on them, a sweet smile on her lips. She was dressed in an ice-blue gown, obviously another of Tony's designs, and the glitter in her eyes told Dany that she was furious. "What an entrance, darling," she exclaimed dulcetly, brushing her cheek against Dany's with spurious affection.

Her armor firmly in place, Dany was able to turn the shaft aside. With a faint smile she murmured, "Hello, Marissa."

The glitter in Marissa's blue eyes increased; she had never been able to get a rise out of Dany, and that enraged her almost beyond bearing. Ignoring the almost ugly man at Dany's side, she said, "Darling, you really must come and meet Bay. I hear he wants you to be in one of his little films! It would be marvelous for you; I told him what a dandy little actress you are!"

Perfectly appreciating the true worth of this artless speech, Dany said with all the calm she could muster, "I've already met him, Marissa."

The blue eyes sharpened with suspicion. "Really? Now, isn't that strange? Just a few minutes ago he told me that he had never met you."

Dany looked down at her glass for a moment, and then lifted her eyes, a queer little smile in them, to Marissa's face. "Perhaps he's forgotten," she said rather dryly.

Marissa's beautiful face immediately assumed the cat-in-the-cream look of satisfaction. She wanted no rivals for Bay's attention, and if he had forgotten about meeting Dany, then obviously she was no rival. With a mechanical smile for Darius she drifted gracefully back toward the fireplace.

"Has he forgotten, Dany?" It was Darius, his voice very quiet.

Dany stared down at her glass rather blindly. "No," she said softly. "No, I don't think he's forgotten."

"I thought not." The violet eyes tracked across the room until they met the thinly veiled hostility of Bay Spencer's gaze. The look between the two men held for a long moment, and even though Darius was not a man to be easily intimidated, he felt a faint flicker of relief that the days of duels were long past. If ever a man looked like he wanted to commit murder! Turning his gaze back to Dany's downbent head, he said gently, "He's the one, isn't he?"

Dany took a quick sip of her drink. "Is it so obvious?" she asked unsteadily.

"To me. But only because I knew there *was* someone." He hesitated, feeling the itch between his shoulders again, and not bothering to wonder who was staring at him. It would be Spencer, of course—just as it had been earlier. "Does he want you for one of his films, Dany?"

"So he says." Dany had recovered her composure; she was able to answer calmly. "I refused, but—he's a very determined man."

"Is that why he's here?"

She raised her head, her veiled eyes looking at Darius without really seeing him. "I think," she replied slowly, "I very much think that he's here because I'm here—and that I'm here because this is where he wanted me to be."

Darius considered this for a moment. A glance showed him that Spencer's attention had been more or less claimed by Marissa, who was clinging to his arm and laughing up at his face. He looked back at the pale, still face of his young friend. "That sounds . . . pretty ruthless."

"Utterly." Dany's smile was a little crooked. "I hope I'm wrong, Darius. I hope he had nothing to with my being here. But it all seems just a little too pat."

"You don't have to stay. I'll talk to Bud if you like—" He broke off as she shook her head determinedly.

"No. Not this time. I've been running for years. I think it's time I stopped."

"You don't want my help, huh?" Darius asked, smiling ruefully.

Dany reached out impulsively to touch his arm. "Thank you, but—but no. I have to see this thing through by myself."

With that odd instinctive understanding that had so much surprised her on the plane, Darius seemed to grasp exactly what she meant. "Okay. But if you ever need me, I'll be here. Don't forget that."

"I won't." Determined to get things back on a normal plane, she went on lightly. "And now—I think I'd better circulate and show off Tony's creation!"

Darius grunted sardonically. "You won't find a single man in this room who doesn't have that dress imprinted on his memory," he told her.

Dany smiled faintly and turned away from him, fixing her mind on the job she was here to do and ignoring everything else. She knew many of the people present, recognizing some of the faces as those belonging to important fashion houses in New York. She moved from group to group, her polite mask firmly in place, being introduced to those people she did not know and talking easily to those she did. She kept her eyes carefully averted from the fireplace, although she was completely aware of Marissa clinging like a limpet to Bay's arm and his dark head bent attentively toward her.

Dany was horrified at the sudden stab of jealousy she felt, helplessly envisioning Marissa's golden body locked in Bay's strong arms. She told herself—not that she cared —that Marissa had failed to enslave Bay once before and that he was certainly too intelligent to be caught in the blonde's trap. Not only did the self-reassurance give her no comfort, it enraged her to think that she cared whether or not Bay fell for Marissa's little tricks.

With her turbulent emotions hidden beneath the mask, Dany continued around the room, pausing at last to exchange a few words with Cy and Susan. "Have you two set the date yet?" she asked.

Susan cast a loving glance at the thin, dark man by her side and said promptly, "January first—and I want you to be my maid of honor." She, too, was wearing one of Tony's creations, a cream gown in a vaguely Grecian style.

In a mournful voice Cy said, "She's making me bide my time until that lousy contract expires. Talk some sense into her, Dany."

Before Dany could respond, dinner was announced, and she followed the couple into the dining room. Her worst fears were realized when she discovered that Bay was seated at her right hand. The man at her left was a stranger to her—the editor of some fashion magazine—and aside from glancing at her dress from time to time with an anticipatory gleam in his eye, he kept his attention strictly on the meal.

Dany, too, attempted to concentrate on the food, trying to ignore the sound of Bay's deep voice as he talked easily to the man on his right. Of the twenty people present only six were women, and Bud had obviously tried to spread them out a little.

"That's quite a dress."

It was Bay, his tone low and mocking, and Dany fought to keep her mask in place. Without looking at him, she said calmly, "I'll tell Tony you said so. I'm sure he'll be flattered." Congratulating herself for not having lost her composure, Dany nearly jumped out of her skin when she felt Bay's hand suddenly grip her upper thigh beneath the table.

Furious green eyes swung immediately to stare into cool blue ones. "Keep your hands to yourself," she hissed, a polite smile pinned to her lips. The hand tightened slightly.

"I told you it wasn't over between us, Dany, and I meant it. I knew you'd run like the little coward you are, so I arranged for you to run here."

Since that possibility had already occurred to her, Dany did not look surprised. Keeping her voice as low as his, and attempting to ignore the warm hand on her leg, she said flatly, "If you don't remove your hand, you'll be

106

sorry." When his only response was a cold smile, Dany made a quick little movement with her right hand, unnoticed by any of the other guests, and Bay's hand drew back rather abruptly, a smothered curse coming from his lips.

He looked down at the four tiny marks on his hand and then at the fork Dany was calmly placing on the table. For a brief moment a glint of honest amusement shone in his eyes. "Resourceful, aren't you?"

"I have terrific survival instincts," she replied coolly. Pointedly she picked up her salad fork and went on with her meal. Bay made no further attempt either to touch her or speak to her, and the meal progressed in silence between them. The other guests didn't seem to notice.

After dinner everyone returned to the great room, and Bud passed around drinks again. This time Dany took only a small glass of sweet sherry, wondering rather desperately how soon she could escape to her room. She mistrusted her ability to maintain her mask under the combined effects of alcohol and Bay's mocking presence, and she wanted the opportunity to sort out her jumbled thoughts in private.

She was denied that luxury, however, since the guests had apparently decided to make a night of it. With her own status being that of a working guest, she knew better than to disappear before her host had released her. It was Tony who finally approached her as she stood talking to Cy and Susan and told her that she should go to bed. Hesitantly she glanced toward the other side of the room. "But won't Bud—"

"He won't mind," Tony interrupted. "Besides," he went on frankly, "you're beginning to look a little strained. It's nearly midnight, and I don't want you to look tired tomorrow; I want you girls to be photographed in the garden in the morning."

Susan laughed. "Well, I like that," she said rather dryly.

"You send Dany off to bed because you don't want her to get too tired, but you don't say a word about Marissa and me!"

In that soft voice that usually forced his listeners to strain in order to hear him, Tony responded calmly, "You have Cy to watch out for you, and Marissa can take care of herself. Dany's so damn polite, she wouldn't think of leaving before someone told her to, so I'm telling her to."

A little surprised at his perceptiveness, Dany smiled at him with real gratitude. Since both Bay and Marissa had been absent from the room for the past half hour, she felt a treacherous desire to burst into tears, and she wanted nothing more than to reach her room and shed them in private. "Thanks, Tony. I think I will turn in."

"Good. Cy, can we start shooting at eight?" He waited for the photographer's nod, then told Dany, "Since we don't want to bother the late sleepers, all the gowns and makeup will be in the music room."

"I didn't know there was one," Dany said in surprise.

"Sure. It's beyond the kitchen in the west wing. Does anybody know where Marissa is? I don't want to have to bang on her door at the crack of dawn."

Susan gazed expressionlessly at her glass. "She disappeared into the garden a few minutes ago with God's gift to women."

Dany stared down at her own glass, feeling the jealousy tearing at her helplessly, and seeing again the vision of the blonde locked in Bay's arms. Tony looked irritated, a faint frown crossing his face. "If she ruins that gown, I'll kill her," he muttered, and headed purposefully toward the garden.

Cy and Susan laughed, but Dany didn't feel very amused. With a faint smile for her friends she murmured a quiet good night and left the room. She walked slowly toward her bedroom, feeling no pleasure as she looked ahead to the next two weeks. Bud had told her that the guests would be coming in batches, staying for a day or two, and then leaving to make way for another group; obviously he planned to entertain the entire New York fashion world before he was through. Darius, she knew, would stay during it all, and Bay as well.

That thought brought a return of the painful jealousy, and Dany was powerless to fight it. The destructive emotion was all mixed up with bitter hatred and bewilderment at the illogical feelings within herself. She shouldn't care that Marissa had got her claws into Bay, but the fact remained that she did care.

Pushing the realization away, Dany stepped into her room and closed the door behind her. As she reached for the light switch she suddenly became aware of the smell of cigarette smoke, and at the same moment, instinct told her that she was not alone in the room. For a moment panic touched her, and then she felt her neck tingle and knew who her unexpected guest was. Nerving herself to face him, she flipped the light switch and looked across the room.

He was sitting in a deep chair by the bed, an ashtray at his elbow. From the contents of the ashtray and the amount of smoke in the room, it was easy to see that he had been waiting for some time. Dany felt sheer relief sweep through her mind as she realized that he had not remained long with Marissa, and was immediately angry at the emotion. Anger won out, and it quivered in her voice when she told him, "Get out of my room."

Bay put his cigarette out casually and rose to his feet. Strolling toward her with that hard, mocking smile on his face, he said calmly, "You and I have a few things to settle, Dany."

"I said, get out!" Her hand fumbled for the doorknob behind her, trying to wrench open the door before he reached her. She had barely managed to get it open a few inches when his hand slammed against the panel above her head, propelling the door closed. Trapped, unable to move because his long hard body was so near, Dany stared up at him.

That metallic, cobalt glitter was in his eyes as he returned the stare, and then his gaze dropped to sweep her body slowly. As it had done earlier in the evening, the look stripped her of everything but the mask, searing her flesh and starting the blood boiling in her veins. She drew in her breath sharply, and his eyes fastened immediately onto her breasts as the gown intensified the gasp.

Trying to fight the feverish desires of her body, Dany said tautly, "You and I have nothing to say to each other."

"You're wrong, Dany," he murmured, his eyes slowly returning to her face in a trail of fire. "We have a great deal to say to each other—but not with words. We don't need words, you and I."

His voice was low and seductive, making her legs weak and her lips tremble uncertainly. God—how had he acquired the hold over her mind, her senses? How could she fight him when her body longed for the passion his eyes promised so vividly? Pride stiffened her backbone suddenly as she asked herself how she would feel when the passion was spent and her life loomed before her, devoid of self-respect. "Get out of my room," she ordered flatly.

His laugh was deep and throaty. "I'm not some callow boy, Dany, infatuated with your beauty and desperate for a kind word. I want you—all of you. And I always get what I want."

"Not this time." Her voice trembled in spite of all her efforts. There had been a deadly certainty in his tone, and she was suddenly aware of her vulnerability where he was concerned. She could tell herself that she hated him, but her body remembered his touch, and her senses quivered with helpless need as she stared up at him.

He laughed again, the sound chilling her. "You may not know what you want, Dany, but I do. You were going crazy in my arms that night."

She stiffened, a wave of heat sweeping up her throat and darkening her cheeks. "Bastard," she whispered with an intensity that surprised them both. "I wouldn't touch you with a barge pole if you were the last man alive!"

His eyes narrowed slightly, studying the bitter hatred glowing in her eyes. "So you hate me, do you?" he murmured thoughtfully. "Well, that's all right. You can hate me all the way to Hell; it doesn't change anything. I can still make you want me, can't I, Dany?"

"No!" she snapped angrily. "God, you have an ego the size of a house! I despise you!"

"But you still want me," he told her calmly.

Her voice heavy with rage and loathing, she said, "The only thing I *want* is for you to leave me alone!"

"Do you, Dany? Do you really?" With cool deliberation he reached out and placed his hand over one of her breasts.

The thin silk of her gown was no protection against the warmth of his hand; her breast responded instantly, swelling and hardening, the nipple rising tautly against his palm. Telling herself fiercely that she wouldn't give him the satisfaction of watching her defend her body's reaction to him, she held on to her mask like a drowning man clutching a tiny piece of driftwood, her hands clenched at her sides. "Go to hell," she told him tightly.

His hand remained on her breast, his eyes darkening. "Tell me now that you don't want me, Dany," he said huskily.

"I don't," she gritted from between clenched teeth. His hand moved slowly, caressingly, and it took every ounce of her willpower to suppress a gasp as dizzying sensations rushed like wildfire through her body.

"Your eyes tell me one thing, but your body tells me something entirely different, Dany. Your heart is beating so fast, I can hardly count it, and your skin is hot, flushed. I could take you right now—you wouldn't even struggle."

The calm certainty in his voice snapped Dany's control. With a cry of rage and pain she moved suddenly, her swinging hand striking his lean cheek with the sound of a gunshot. It was an impulsive, instinctive movement; she could no longer bear his certainty or her own weakness.

Her wrist was caught in a viselike grip, her body jerked abruptly against the unyielding length of his. "That was a mistake, sweetheart," he told her grimly, his cheek bearing the outline of her fingers. "I don't allow anyone to hit me and go unpunished for it!" His head descended, his lips finding hers in a savage, brutal kiss.

Her head whirling, Dany managed to keep her mouth closed against his, twisting and turning in a useless attempt to escape the cruel embrace. His arms were like iron bars, his hard body burning against hers, as though the fire within his mind were scorching his flesh as well. She had never felt such intense fury emanating from another human being in her life. His hard lips crushed hers, punishing, demanding. Her soft inner lip was torn against her teeth, and when the coppery taste of blood filled her mouth, she released a ragged moan and surrendered, her body going limp in his arms and her lips parting at last.

Immediately he deepened the barbaric kiss, his tongue an alien intruder. He seemed intent on drawing the very soul from her body, a raw burning hunger in the mouth moving over hers, the hands caressing her roughly. Suddenly tearing his lips from hers, he whirled her about and flung her across the bed, nearly pulling her arm from its socket.

112

Dany landed in a breathless heap on the bed, shock keeping her still for those few precious seconds during which she might have escaped. And then the heavy weight of his body covered hers, and she was helpless again. The moment his lips reclaimed hers, what little strength she possessed deserted her. Desire gripped her in its merciless talons, stealing away her will. A kaleidoscope of impressions burst onto her senses: the sensually abrasive touch of his hands, the spicy scent of his after-shave, the brandy taste of his mouth.

A last flicker of sanity made her raise her hands to his shoulders in an attempt to push him away, and she tore her lips from him to utter a shaken plea. "No! Please, Bay. Don't do this!"

Ignoring the plea—if he heard it at all—he caught her wrists in an iron grip and stretched her arms up over her head, pinning them to the bed. His mouth ravaged the soft skin of her throat, his lips burning, shaking. His free hand pulled the pins from her hair and spread it out over her white shoulder, and then moved slowly to push down the bodice of the silky gown. The hard mouth immediately followed his hand, exploring the silken valley, the rosy peaks.

The violence within him had not abated; it seemed, instead, to be growing ever more powerful with every passing second. His lean body was taut and pulsing with desire, his hands and lips hard and hot. One knee thrust itself between her thighs, the powerful strength of it easily overcoming her instinctive resistance.

Dany felt her last grip on reason slip away into a ruby void. Her senses flared with a pleasure that was almost agony; she closed her eyes as a shaking moan left her throat. Nothing in the world was real except the emotions splintering through her body, the hands and lips teasing her to incredible heights of pleasure. Biting lips already

113

bruised and swollen, she turned her head from side to side restlessly, her body shuddering beneath the heavy weight of his. The void within her body was growing, expanding, until it seemed to her dazed mind that she was one big empty ache.

His hot lips against her breast, Bay muttered fiercely, "Did Carrington make you go crazy like this, Dany? And the other one—Tremaine—did he? Do you respond to them like this?"

Green eyes darkened almost to jet opened and stared at him in confusion. "What? I don't—"

The hand resting on her thigh came up suddenly to tangle in the thickness of her hair, jerking her head back as he lifted his own head and stared down at her with the fires of hell in his eyes. "Answer me!" he commanded harshly. "Have they seen you like this?"

Her eyes watering from the pain of his cruel grip, Dany cried softly, "No! They haven't—"

His mouth abruptly cut off the rest of her words, closing over her own with intense hunger. The brutal kiss went on and on, taking and taking until there was nothing left. When at last he raised his head, he was breathing heavily. "I could take you right now, Dany. You know that."

She stared up at him like a rabbit in a snare; her only defense against him was the mask that hid her thoughts. Her breathing was rapid, shallow; her body was still trembling beneath him.

"I could take you—but I won't." His face moved closer to hers, an odd, fixed expression in his metallic eyes. "I'm going to wait, Dany, until I know that your surrender is complete. Then I'll take you."

"What?" she whispered, suddenly frightened by the very quietness of his voice.

"The mask." Softly, implacably, he went on. "I'll destroy that mask if I have to kill you to do it. You'll be stripped bare, Dany, helpless. And then I'll make you mine."

Sickened, Dany turned her face away, the color of shame sweeping over her face as she remembered the way she had responded to him. God, she hated him! And, worse than that—she hated herself.

The heavy weight of his body was removed suddenly, and Dany immediately turned on her side away from him. She heard him move to the door, and then the tingle on her neck told her that he had looked back at her.

"By the way—I've discovered that I don't want you for the film after all. I'll find another Serena. After I've finished with you, of course!" When her only response was silence, he laughed harshly and left the room.

Dany lay there for a long time, and then slowly slid off the bed. She crossed to the door and locked it with shaking fingers. Like a robot, she stripped off the emerald gown and threw it on the bed before going into her bathroom and turning on the shower. She made the water as hot as she could stand it, scrubbing her body until the flesh was pink and glowing. Only then did she step from the bath.

Drying herself, she glanced into the mirror over the vanity and froze in sudden horror, the numbness gone from her mind. She looked as though someone had been beating her. Her lips were swollen and discolored; faint bruises were beginning to form on her throat and breasts; the marks of Bay's fingers showed plainly on her wrists. Oh, God! By morning she'd be livid; she always bruised easily.

Avoiding her mirrored image, Dany quickly dressed in a long gown hanging on the back of the bathroom door, her hands shaking uncontrollably. What would she tell everyone?

She went into the bedroom and sank down in the chair by her bed and glanced at the travel clock on the nightstand. It was after one. That meant that she was due to pose for photos in the garden in less than six hours. She remembered photographers in the past who had raised holy hell because she had fallen off a horse or run into something, bruising her pale skin. Within hours she would be a virtual rainbow of colors, and it would take days for them to fade. And make up wouldn't cover the bruises.

She felt sick with shame at how nearly she had come to giving in to Bay. Nearly! That was almost funny. She *had* given in. Even knowing that his only desire was for her body, she had given in. She thought back to the day she had first realized that she loved him, remembered her shock at the realization that she was drawn to something dark and primitive inside him. It was true. His passion toward her tonight had been brutal, and something within her had responded helplessly to that savagery.

Dany dropped her hot face into her hands, wishing vainly that she could cry. A bitter bile rose in her throat as she acknowledged yet another loss to this man—a man who thought her a tramp. First it had been her heart; tonight it had been her body. She had offered herself to him helplessly, unable to deny the need she felt for him, and he had rejected her—because her body wasn't *enough*. He wanted everything. Everything inside her. He would take it all, because she had dared to withhold from him the secrets of her mind.

It was a frightening thought. He was driven by a dark, obsessive desire to see her beaten and helpless. He wanted to hear her beg for his possession, hear her cry out her need and her love.

Love? Dany pushed the thought away. Not love. Just need. Just? God! As if that wasn't enough. A need that tortured her body and mind and left her helpless in the cruel arms of a man she bitterly hated.

CHAPTER SEVEN

Dany was still sitting in the chair, the drapes drawn against the morning light, when there was a soft knock on her door at a quarter past eight.

"Dany?" It was Tony, his soft voice barely reaching her ears. "Dany, it's after eight. The rest of them are waiting in the garden."

Her light was on; she couldn't pretend to be asleep. "I can't make it today, Tony. I—I'm sorry."

There was a moment of silence. "Why not? What's wrong, Dany?"

"Nothing. I just . . . don't feel very well, that's all."

Another silence. "Open the door, Dany, I want to talk to you."

"Tony, please. I don't want to see anyone. We can take care of my shots later in the week, can't we?"

He was silent for so long that Dany began to hope he had gone away, but then his voice came, very quiet. "Dany, if you don't open this door right now, I'm going to wake Bud up and ask him where the key is."

Shrugging with weary defeat, Dany murmured, "Just a

minute." She went to the closet and found her terry robe, pulling it on over the cream nightgown and tying the belt securely. She took a moment to run a brush through her hair, then went to open the door.

Tony stepped inside the room, his mouth open to speak. Without making a sound, however, his mouth slowly closed as the dark eyes took in her appearance. Her lips were swollen and nearly purple; vivid bruises marked her throat and her wrists. Everything else was covered, but Tony could well imagine what the rest of her body must look like. Quickly he closed the door and leaned back against it, his face grim. "My God, Dany—"

She made a helpless little gesture. "I'm not very photogenic, am I?"

"What happened? Or is that a dumb question?"

Dany moved over to sit on the bed, her eyes shadowed with weariness. "Nothing happened. At least—not what you can be forgiven for thinking. I just bruise easily, that's all."

"With that white skin you probably do," he agreed, his face still grim. "Be that as it may, it still took some pretty rough handling to mark you like that." His gaze fell on the heap of emerald silk on the bed. A soft oath burst from his lips. "That damn dress! Dany, I swear I didn't think anything like this would happen—"

"It wasn't the dress," she interrupted firmly. "Believe me, Tony, it wasn't the dress."

A certain measure of relief entered his dark eyes, but he still looked grim. "There's a bastard under this roof, and he ought to be shot!" Tony's voice sounded surprisingly violent.

Dany shook her head quickly. "Please, Tony. I don't want anyone to know about—about this. It isn't as bad as it looks." The bruised lips moved in a weak smile. "It's

118

just that I feel as if I've got a scarlet *A* painted on my breast."

"Damm it, if one of the guests—"

"Please, Tony. Don't say anything. To anyone."

He stared at her for a long moment. "Just tell me one thing—truthfully. Did he hurt you?"

Dany knew what he was asking; she met his eyes squarely. "No. He didn't hurt me."

After a moment he nodded slowly. "All right. I won't say anything—this time. But if it happens again, I'll pull out all the stops, Dany."

She accepted the warning calmly. "Just tell the others that I've caught some kind of bug and don't want to be disturbed today. And, Tony . . . thanks."

His mouth twisted wryly. "Sure." He turned to open the door and then hesitated. Looking back over his shoulder, he asked quietly, "Who was it, Dany?"

"I'll take care of it myself, Tony. I don't want anyone else involved."

He nodded, as if half expecting the response, and then silently left the room. Dany rose from the bed and went over to lock the door. Returning to the bed, she curled up on her side and stared at the wall, eyes burning with exhaustion in her pale face. She was so tired. So tired. . . .

It was afternoon when she awoke to hear a soft tapping on her door and Susan's voice calling to her.

"Dany? I know you don't feel well, but you have to eat; I've brought a tray for you."

Dany's stomach shied nervously away from the thought of eating—and the thought of facing Susan. She wanted no one else to see the bruises she was wearing like a badge of shame. She remained silent and, after a time, Susan went away.

Dany slept off and on during the afternoon, the periods of sleep restless and filled with frightening dreams, the waking moments full of bitter thoughts.

She was awake when another knock fell on her door sometime after dark. She remained silent, determined to see no one, but then Tony's soft voice reached her.

"It's me, Dany. Open the door; I've brought you something to eat."

Dany slid from the bed and went to the door, drawing the lapels of her robe closer together and tightening the belt. Pushing her hair over her shoulder, she unlocked the door and opened it. Tony came in, carrying a tray.

He shot a penetrating glance at her and then nodded toward the chair by her bed. "You'd better sit there; it'll be easier for you to hold the tray. And before you say anything, I've got orders to see that you eat every bite."

Dany crossed the room and sank down in the chair with a faint smile. "Orders? From whom?"

"Everyone," Tony replied dryly, coming over to place the tray in her lap. "You've got 'em all worried to death."

She frowned as she stared down at the cheese omelet and bowl of fragrant chicken soup. "I didn't mean to worry anyone," she murmured, picking up a spoon and beginning to eat the soup.

Tony sat down on the foot of her bed and regarded her with a faint smile. "I'll tell them that you're feeling much better, and they'll be satisfied. You certainly look better." His smile deepened as she looked up in surprise. "Oh, not as far as the bruises go; they look like a Technicolor nightmare. But your mouth isn't as swollen as it was, and you don't look as tired and—brittle as you did this morning."

Dany raised her glass of milk in a rueful toast and then sipped it slowly. "I heard quite a bit of noise this afternoon. More guests?"

120

"No, that was last night's bunch leaving. There was a change of plans or something, so the next group won't arrive until tomorrow afternoon."

She set her glass on the tray and carefully tasted the omelet, wondering absently how much her churning stomach could bear. "By then I should be able to cover most of the bruises with makeup."

"You're beginning to look a little green," Tony observed.

Dany rather hastily covered the omelet with her napkin and concentrated on the soup. "I'm a little queasy, that's all. It'll pass." She looked up and found him watching her narrowly. "And I'm not pregnant, if that's what you're thinking."

Tony looked surprised. "That wasn't what I was thinking; I know you aren't pregnant."

It was Dany's turn to look surprised. "Now, how in the world could you know that?"

He stared at her for a moment, the dark brows lifting. "Susan told me you weren't aware of it," he murmured thoughtfully, "but I didn't see how that could be."

Bewildered, she asked, "Tony, what are you talking about?"

"Dany," he said slowly, "don't you see what it is that's made you such a famous model? Don't you realize what people see when they look at you?"

"I . . . never really thought about it. I guess they see what they want to see."

"They see your eyes."

Dany gazed at him blankly. "Well, of course they see my eyes. But—"

He held up a hand to halt her. "Innocence, Dany. When people look at you, they see innocence in your eyes. That's why men are drawn to you so powerfully. All that beautiful, seductive innocence drives them out of their minds.

121

The conquering instinct and all that. Each man wants to be the one to teach you—the secrets of life, and watch that innocence turn to knowledge."

Stunned, she could only stare at him, her mind whirling with this new thought. The reactions of men toward her had baffled her for years, the intensity of their stares making her nervous and wary. She had never understood what they saw when they looked at her. But now . . .

Tony grinned faintly. "Don't think I'm making a pass; I have a fiancée in New York who keeps me pretty happy. But I like you, Dany. I don't want to see you get hurt."

Dany leaned over to place the almost untouched tray on the bed. "Thanks for telling me, Tony. It—explains a few things I didn't understand."

He looked down at the tray for a moment and then picked it up and got to his feet. "Be careful, Dany," he warned quietly. "I've known men to become obsessed with innocence like yours."

Dany nodded silently, trying to ignore her sudden chill of fear. In a very quiet voice she murmured, "I've learned more about myself in the past few days than I have in my whole lifetime. It's a lot to think about."

"Sometimes it happens that way," he told her gently. "You spend half your life behind a curtain without even being aware of it, and then something happens to rip the curtain away."

Dany's bruised lips quirked in a faint sad smile. "I know what you mean."

Tony went toward the door and then hesitated. "Spencer's a powerful man," he said in an expressionless voice. "He could hurt your career and mine as well, but don't let that fear keep you here, Dany. If Bud knew what had happened, he'd throw the bastard out on his ear—friend or no friend."

"How did you—"

"When I told the others that you weren't feeling well, Spencer was the only one—aside from Marissa—who didn't look concerned."

In a bitter voice Dany said, "He wouldn't be! But I'm not going to run away, Tony. My mind went round and round in frantic circles all night, but that's finished now, and I won't let him use me. It might tear me to pieces inside, but he's not going to walk away from me with another notch on his belt!"

The tangled, emotional speech appeared to make some kind of sense to Tony, for he nodded slowly. "I thought there was a spirited lady underneath all that glamor," he said with a flickering smile, and then silently left the room.

Dany didn't bother to lock the door after him. Instead, she rose and crossed to the mirror above the dresser. Wide green eyes, dark and disturbed, returned her stare. There were no thoughts to be read there, only bitter pain and raging anger. Was that what Bay saw when he looked into her eyes? Was that why he was so grimly determined to strip away her mask?

But why? For God's sake—*why*? What had she ever done to him that he should want to hurt her so badly? She would have given him everything if he had not made his contempt for her so blatantly apparent. But he had, and she had drawn away from him. Had she wounded his pride, perhaps? No, that didn't make sense. On that awful night when Jason had called, it had been more than wounded pride that had made him rage at her.

Until then he had been so kind to her. Pretence or not, he had charmed her and teased her until she had fallen in love with him. But then Jason had called and . . . what? He had been angry *because* of the call. His fury had been strangely bitter, as if she had somehow hurt him.

Dany moved slowly back to her chair, her brow furrowed in thought. Sinking down, she focused her mind on the night before. At the height of that stormy interlude he had demanded fiercely if other men in her life had had the power to make her feel the way that he could. That was . . . odd. It was almost as if he had been jealous of the mythical love affairs in her past.

Jealous? Was jealousy behind his obsession to see her protective mask stripped away? Did he possess some dark need to see her vulnerable as no man had seen her before?

A part of Dany accepted that possibility, but another part of her felt that there was something more to it. He wanted to hurt her, to destroy her. Even his most passionate caresses had been riddled with contempt; he had looked at her with scorn as well as desire. *Why?*

Since first realizing her love for him, she had been aware of violent emotions seething within him, a primitive savagery that both attracted and repelled her. On the surface he seemed calm, but she knew how deceptive and brittle that calm was. Like a slumbering volcano, he was capable of erupting without warning, pouring bitter ash over the object of his anger.

And she was cursed with the ability to draw that anger, God knew why. At times he seemed to hate her, and yet his passion for her was real. She had been aware of his body, taut and trembling above her last night; aware of the shaking desire of his mouth against her flesh. Was it possible to love and hate at the same time?

The question brought Dany's head up with a snap. God! Wasn't that the painful state of her own emotions at this very moment? She loved him and hated him and wanted to hurt him because he had hurt her. But Bay didn't love her. Blind to the innocence that Tony had described, Bay thought her a tramp. But he wanted her.

With a tired sigh Dany pushed the bewildering questions out of her mind. She took a shower and washed her long hair, then sat in her darkened bedroom with only the

124

faint glow from a lamp on the nightstand lighting the room. She sat in the shadows and brushed her hair while it dried, the slow steady movements bringing a sort of quiet to her troubled mind. She was wearing her terry robe over a fresh nightgown, her feet bare and tucked beneath her in the chair.

Hours passed. She heard the faint sounds of the others coming and going in the hall outside her door, but by midnight the house was quiet. Dany tossed her brush on the bed and then turned frowning eyes to the door, some instinct telling her that there was someone in the hall. Her breath caught in her throat as she watched the doorknob turning, and then the door opened and Bay stepped into the room, closing the door behind him.

Sheer rage swept through Dany. She jumped to her feet, the lamp behind her presenting an entrancing silhouette to the man who had just entered the room. "You have no right to walk into my room without knocking!"

Bay, in a casual shirt unbuttoned almost to the waist and dark slacks that emphasized the lean strength of his legs, laughed mockingly. "I'll come in here anytime I want to, Dany. How long are you going to sulk like a spoiled brat? Just because I made you face how you feel—"

"I'm not sulking!"

"Oh, no?" The mocking laugh sounded again. "Pretending to be ill and hiding in your room all day sounds like sulking to me. Were you planning on hiding for the next two weeks?"

There was a long silence, and then, in a flat voice, Dany said, "If that's how long it takes. Turn on the light, Bay."

He stared at her, frowning. "What?"

"Turn on the light. There's something I want you to see."

Still frowning, he turned to flip the switch by the door, and then turned back to face her as bright light filled the room. What he saw drained the color from his face. Her green eyes were haunted with bitter pain, the faint purple shadows beneath them mutely attesting to her exhaustion. The tender lips were discolored, the slender throat marked with savage bruises. He watched, stunned, as she lifted one wrist and shook back the cuff of her robe to expose the purplish marks of his fingers on the white skin.

"This is why I've been *hiding* in my room all day. If I had gone out looking like this, do you know what the others would have thought? That I'd been raped! And they wouldn't have been far wrong, would they, Bay? Except for a slight technicality, that's exactly what happened!"

Bay's eyes darkened; remorse and horror quivered in his voice as he whispered, "My God. . . . Did I do that?"

"Oh, no!" Dany was too bitter to care what she was saying, she was only aware of a twisted desire to hurt him. "My bedroom has a revolving door, didn't you know? Men come and go at all hours; it's amazing how I keep up with them!" She laughed mirthlessly. "Of course, last night was a bit too much—"

"Don't!" he interrupted, his voice a hoarse, strangled sound, his face dead white.

"Why?" she shot back furiously. "It's what you think! It's what you've thought from the first!"

"That isn't true!"

She laughed again, a terrible sound in the quiet room. "God, do you think I didn't see the contempt in your eyes? I saw it, all right. But you should turn that contempt on yourself. You're nothing but an animal!"

He winced. "I never meant to hurt you."

Dany was still too angry to hear the pain in his voice, to see the remorse in his eyes. "You wanted to *destroy* me—to take everything from me until only a hollow shell was left!"

"No!" He raked an unsteady hand through his black

126

hair, his expression a far cry from the mocking one he had worn when he had first entered the room. "I'd had too much to drink, and I saw red when you slapped me—but I never meant to do that to you. You've been driving me crazy since the day we met; I wanted you so much I just lost control."

"Want!" she mocked bitterly. Her hand raised abruptly to pull aside the lapel of her robe, exposing the vivid bruises marring the curve of one white breast. "What does that look like, Bay? Marks of passion? Desire? No! They're marks of hate. You don't *want* me, Bay—you want to break me!"

"No—I—"

"You said as much last night!" She pulled the robe back into place, staring at him angrily. "You said you wanted me stripped bare—helpless! Does that sound like desire? No; it's hate. Well, you can spend the rest of your life hating women if you want to!" The words were uttered by sheer instinct; Dany seemed to have no control over her own tongue.

"I've done nothing to earn your contempt, and I'll be *damned* if I'll stand here and take it! Fling your insults at other women, punish them for some wrong you created in your own mind—but leave me out of it! I won't let you destroy me, Bay!"

His face was gray; an oddly stricken look appeared in his indigo eyes as he stared at her. Some terrible struggle seemed to be taking place within him, and every muscle in his body was knotted with tension. "You don't know what you're talking about," he bit out hoarsely.

"Don't I?" As pale as he was, Dany stared at him, convinced that her instinctively hurled accusation had struck a nerve. Blind intuition had prompted her to make a wild stab in the dark, and his reaction confirmed her guess. At some point in his life, Bay had been badly hurt by a woman, and it had twisted something inside of him. After her rage evaporated, Dany said quietly, "I won't let you hurt me."

Their eyes locked together for a long moment, hers still veiled against him, his uncertain for the first time. Then, with a savage curse, he left the room, slamming the door violently behind him.

Dany stood where she was for a long time, silently acknowledging to herself that her hatred for Bay had been lost somewhere during the brief, stormy encounter between them. Even her bitterness seemed to have seeped away. Sadly she wondered if he was capable of trusting a woman, or if he would always feel a desire to hurt before he himself could be hurt.

Throwing herself across the bed, she cried bitterly for the starving love within her. Her hatred for him had been a fragile thing, born in a moment of bitter pain and never as strong as she had believed it to be. But her love for him had crept in silently, rooting itself firmly in her heart and clinging there with tenacity. She could neither fight it nor reject it.

She loved him. She loved a man who had shown her contempt, who had sneered at her, who believed her to be a tramp. She loved a man whose own twisted nature could never allow him to return that love . . . even if he wanted to.

By morning the bruises had faded a little. Dany had resorted to taking a sleeping pill some time after Bay had stormed from the room, and when her alarm went off at eight, she rolled over groggily to shut it off, gritting her teeth against the reverberations of the shrill sound in her head. A hot shower helped to dispel the drug-induced cobwebs, and by the time she was trying to decide what to wear, she felt reasonably awake.

128

A bright lipstick had disguised the faintly bruised appearance of her mouth; a long-sleeved western-style shirt, with only the top button left open, hid most of the other bruises. By the time she had spent ten minutes with her makeup case, she had managed to hide all but one of the bluish marks on her throat.

Staring at the one remaining bruise at the base of her throat, Dany helplessly remembered Bay's lips pressed urgently to that spot, and something quivered inside her. Hastily she tore her eyes from the mirror and bent to rummage in a dresser drawer. Within moments she had wound a scarf around her neck, tying it in a western style to match her shirt. That, along with her close-fitting blue jeans, made her look as if she were on her way to a rodeo, but since the western look was in, Dany didn't worry about it.

She slipped her feet into casual shoes and headed for the dining room, resolutely pushing Bay from her mind. That resolution, however, didn't do much good when she entered the dining room to find that he was the only occupant.

He was sitting in lonely splendor at one side of the long table, a cup of coffee in front of him and his frowning gaze fixed on the table. He looked tired, as if he hadn't slept very much, and whatever his thoughts were, they were obviously not happy ones.

Dany's first impulse was to turn and run, but she managed to overcome the cowardly thought. She went instead to the sideboard and poured herself a cup of coffee, the warning tingle telling her that he had become aware of her entrance.

"Good morning." His voice was quiet.

Dany busied herself inspecting the covered dishes on the sideboard and held on to her mask grimly. "Good morning," she replied calmly. Her appetite having deserted her, Dany settled on a couple of pieces of toast. She carried these, along with her coffee, to the table and seated herself some distance from him, trying to ignore his presence.

"Dany, about the other night—"

She bent her head so that her hair fell forward to hide most of her face from him. "I'd rather not talk about it if you don't mind."

"For God's sake, at least let me apologize," he exclaimed in a low, taut voice. "Dany, I know you didn't believe what I said last night, but I swear, I never meant to hurt you."

"All right," she responded distantly. "You never meant to hurt me. Now can we drop the subject, please?"

"You still don't believe me," he declared huskily.

She raised veiled eyes to stare across the table at him, one delicate brow rising slightly. "It's a little hard to when I look in the mirror." Immediately she had a sick feeling of shame when she saw the color drain from his face, and she wondered tormentedly why she still possessed this awful desire to hurt him.

"I'm sorry." His voice was so low, she had to strain to hear it. "I know that doesn't change anything, but I am sorry, Dany. I've made you hate me, haven't I?"

"I told you that." She had to grit her teeth to keep from telling him that she didn't hate him at all; only the knowledge that her admission of love would be a powerful weapon in his hands kept her silent. She didn't trust him.

"I know. I—I didn't believe you at first. I thought you were just saying it because you didn't like the way I made you feel." He made a quick dismissing gesture with one hand. "Forget I said that. Physical desire has nothing to do with emotions, I know."

"I'm sure you do," she returned flatly, her voice successfully hiding the amazement she felt. He really believed that! He really believed that sexual attraction had nothing to do with emotion!

He went on, his voice strained. "I realized last night that you really do hate me. God knows, I've given you reason. Those bruises . . ."

Another little shock quivered in Dany as she stared at his taut face. He was ashamed of himself. The man who was well-known for his utterly ruthless nature was actually ashamed of himself. Dany took a deep breath, knowing that she had to set his mind at ease. He couldn't know that she bruised with ridiculous ease; couldn't know that, for all his roughness, he had not actually hurt her. But before she could speak, his voice reached her ears.

"I don't blame you for hating me; I'm not too crazy about myself at the moment. But you don't have to worry —I won't bother you anymore." On this bitter exclamation he rose from his chair and quickly left the room.

Dany sat where she was, staring down at her coffee cup. She wanted to go after him and tell him the truth—that the bruises had looked much worse than they actually were—but something held her back. If she told him—if she removed the reason for his remorse—his seductive attitude toward her might well return. He still wanted her; the mutual desire they felt had been an almost tangible thing, quivering in the air between them. She could deal with her own need as long as she stayed away from him, but once in his arms, the slender thread of control would swiftly desert her, she knew.

No. . . . He would have to go on believing that he really had hurt her. It was the only way.

The next three days passed quickly. A new group of fashion and advertising people arrived, and Dany found herself modeling one beautiful creation after another for them. With her polite mask firmly in place she smiled and talked easily to the guests, posed for Cy's camera, and generally performed the duties she'd been hired for.

The bruises faded until they were only memories, and she no longer needed to resort to makeup to cover them. The days settled into a routine of sorts, and if Dany's smile seemed a little brittle at times, apparently no one noticed.

Of Bay she saw very little. He always gathered in the great room with the other guests before and after dinner, but he never spoke to her except in passing and his remarks were always casual. He seemed to be devoting himself entirely to Marissa, and the blonde was purring like a cat.

Dany could only assume that it was Marissa who was keeping him at the lodge, and that realization brought a stabbing pain to her heart. The hardest thing she had ever had to do in her life was to pretend disinterest at the sight of Marissa smiling up at Bay seductively. Occasionally she would feel a slight tingle on her neck, but whenever she shot a veiled glance at Bay, she would see him smiling down at Marissa with faintly mocking charm.

How wrong the poets were! Love wasn't a sweet, fragile thing at all. It was a bitter, tearing emotion that came like a thief in the night to plunder the heart. It stole pride and self-respect, leaving only a shell to ache with emptiness.

Dany tossed in her bed at night with that awful ache; her dreams were haunted with memories of Bay's touch. She would wake after those dreams to find her heart thudding painfully, and her body hot and trembling.

Once she woke to the realization that her pillow was wet with tears, the ache inside her more pronounced than ever; and the memory of holding a black-haired, blue-eyed baby in her arms kept her awake for the rest of the night.

CHAPTER EIGHT

Dany wandered in the garden aimlessly, feeling lost and alone. It was just after dawn; dew glimmered wetly on the bushes and flowers surrounding her, but she took no notice of the early morning beauty. With a faint sigh, she pushed her hands into the pockets of her jeans and walked slowly along the winding path, head bent. She loved this garden. The tall hedges made it seem a private, secret place. It was easy to forget that it was virtually surrounded by the lodge.

She thought back to the night before, and another sigh left her. The painful dream she had awakened to had been the culmination of a night of sheer tension. Several fashion reporters had been present for the evening, and more than one had made snide comments to Dany about her supposed relationship with Jason. Smiling, Dany allowed the shafts to roll off her threadbare armor, tension filling her as she realized that Bay had heard the comments. She had felt him watching her several times, but whenever she glanced his way, it was to find him apparently occupied with Marissa.

Dany had finally taken refuge at Darius's side, secure in the belief that he could handle sarcasm from the reporters much easier than she could. This belief was well founded; she watched him make mincemeat of three different reporters during the remainder of the evening.

Pushing the memory from her mind, Dany continued along the path until she came to her favorite place. It was in the center of the garden, the winding, mazelike hedges providing access from several different directions. The focal point, at least in Dany's mind, of the entire garden was here. Two giant horses, rearing away from each other and sculpted entirely from hedges, occupied the central position of the garden. The detail was incredible; from a distance they seemed living animals. Roses grew profusely about their churning hooves.

The rock-lined gravel path completely encircled the leafy steeds, with stone benches placed at convenient points. Dany had spent many hours here, with only the horses for company.

Involuntarily she smiled as she came upon them, impressed, as she always was, by the artistic genius of some unknown person. She made a mental note to ask Bud who was responsible for creating the creatures and began to move around the path to her particular bench. She came to an abrupt halt, however, when she realized that her bench was occupied.

Bay sat there, leaning back against the tree growing just behind the bench, his long legs stretched out in front of him. The stubs of numerous cigarettes littered the gravel in front of him; another burned between his fingers. His brooding gaze was bent on the hedge-horses; a bluish growth of beard darkened his lean jaw. Dany received the distinct impression that he had been there all night.

She drew a startled breath and he immediately looked up, his eyes darkening as he saw her. The garden was wrapped in an early morning mist, and she seemed to him a shy, fey creature with her copper-gold hair flowing about her shoulders and her slender body poised as if for flight. The green eyes were wide and wary; her expression, uncertain.

He threw his cigarette to the ground and stood up, his leanly powerful body oddly formidable in the stillness of the garden. "Good morning. You're up early," he said quietly.

Unwilling somehow to let him know that her sleep had been disturbed, she managed to reply calmly, "I like walking here in the mornings. I'm sorry—I didn't mean to disturb you."

"You didn't."

Strangely breathless beneath his intent look, Dany turned her own eyes to the roses, feeling tension vibrating in the air between them.

"Those reporters last night," he said suddenly. "They upset you, didn't they?"

"I—what do you mean?" she asked almost inaudibly.

He moved a little closer to her, frowning. "They were making cracks about you and Carrington, asking questions. It bothered you."

A brief smile flitted across her lips and was gone. "I should be used to it by now." She wondered if her mask was weakening, or if he was simply becoming more perceptive.

"You told me once that those rumors were lies." It sounded like a question.

"Yes, I did," she answered levelly.

"Why don't you tell them that?"

Dany sighed. "They wouldn't have believed me."

"Why not?"

"Don't be obtuse!" she snapped suddenly, her nerves frayed. "I could show them a doctor's report stating flatly that I'm a bona fide virgin, and they still wouldn't believe me!"

There was a moment of silence; she still refused to look at him. "So you just try to ignore them."

"Yes."

"Haven't you ever heard that silence gives assent?" His voice was rough.

"And if I defended myself?" She shot one quick look at him, her green eyes bitter, then stared at the roses. "They still wouldn't believe me—any more than you did."

"How was I supposed to believe it after Carrington called?" he asked harshly. "You told him that something wasn't finished, that you needed more time. What could it have been except an affair?"

"It wasn't an affair. It was . . . something else."

"What?" he demanded fiercely. "What were you talking about, Dany?"

She wanted to tell him about her book, but a wall built during five years of silence was not an easy thing to breech, and she was unable to form the words. "It doesn't matter," she said dully. "You'll believe what you want to believe."

Silence stretched tautly between them; only the soft twitter of birds broke the stillness. Dany began to fiddle absently with a red rose in front of her, wondering when Bay would walk off and leave her alone with her painful thoughts.

But he didn't move. After a long moment he said, "I'm sorry. It isn't any of my business, is it?" His voice was tight, strained.

Dany bent her head, allowing the copper-gold hair to fall forward and hide her face. "No. It isn't."

"Is it Tremaine's business?" The question seemed torn from him against his will.

"Darius is my friend."

"Like Carrington." He laughed shortly.

"Like Jason," she agreed flatly. "And you can read anything into that you want. You will anyway."

She had been toying with the rose absently, and since all her concentration was on what they were saying, she forgot to take care with the thorns. A soft cry broke from her suddenly and she pulled her hand back to see a small dot of blood welling up on her index finger. Instinctively she started to move the injured finger to her mouth, but Bay was quicker.

His large hand caught hers in a gentle clasp, carrying it to his mouth and pressing his lips to the bleeding finger. Dany's heart seemed to stop beating for an eternal moment, and then began to pound painfully as she felt his tongue moving against the pad of her finger. It was an incredibly sensuous gesture, tender and moving, and she lifted darkening eyes to stare at him, the breath catching in her throat.

His dark head was bent over her hand, the eyes veiled with heavy lids, all his attention focused on what he was doing. He didn't content himself with only the wounded finger, but pressed his lips to each one in turn in a gesture at once cherishing and passionate. At last his mouth moved to her soft palm, the lips warm and firm, his tongue probing sensuously.

Dany's fingers quivered against his beard-roughened cheek, her breath came quickly from between slightly parted lips. She made no move to pull away, no move to stop him.

He lifted his head at last to stare at her with disturbed indigo eyes. "Don't look at me like that," he said huskily.

"Like what?" she whispered, unaware of the shimmering darkness of her eyes.

His free hand came out slowly to brush a strand of her hair away from her cheek. "Like that," he murmured, gazing into her eyes. "I can't think straight when you look at me like that. I just want to carry you away somewhere and make love to you for a week. Or a year."

The husky words were a potent seduction, and Dany felt her legs weaken and begin to tremble. She forgot the bitter emotions between them, forgot that she had promised herself that she would stay away from him, forgot that he didn't love her. The desire she felt for him was a living thing inside her, consuming her will.

He groaned suddenly, his eyes darkening almost to black. "Oh, God, Dany," he muttered hoarsely, his hands reaching out gently to frame her face. "I have to—hate me later, but I have to. . . ."

His lips touched hers with shattering tenderness, the passion she could feel within him held rigidly in check. It was the most gentle kiss they had ever exchanged, and Dany stood perfectly still, unwilling to make any move that might have disturbed the fragility of this magical moment. Her eyes closed, and she felt all her senses come to quivering life as his mouth moved softly over hers.

Her lips slackened and began to tremble, and still he made no move to deepen the kiss. It was as if he held a tiny bird within his hands, fragile and wary, and did not want to frighten it. His tongue gently probed the soft inner flesh of her lips, his fingers slid down to softly imprison her throat. One thumb moved caressingly over the pulse beating frantically just below her ear.

When the kiss finally deepened to passion, it was not a fierce demand but a slow, insidious assault on her senses, the very tenderness of it robbing her of her last mental reservation. Her mouth bloomed beneath his, her tongue making a tentative exploration of its own, and he groaned deep in his throat.

Bay carried her hands to his chest, murmuring against her mouth, "Touch me, Dany. I need you to touch me."

It was beyond Dany's power to ignore the husky command, and she obeyed mindlessly, her trembling fingers unfastening the buttons of his shirt so that she could touch the strong, hair-roughened chest. Feverishly her hands moved over the taut muscles, feeling his heart pounding heavily beneath her touch, his breathing quicken.

One strong hand slid down her back to her hips, pulling her against his hard length so that she could feel his urgent desire, making her even more aware of her own hollow, aching need. She felt his other hand parting the buttons of her blouse, seeking the warm white flesh beneath it, still with that odd, shaking gentleness. The lacy cup of her bra was pushed aside and his hand caressed her breast with butterfly softness, tracing the swelling curve, the hardening peak.

Every nerve in Dany's body seemed to shatter at that moment; sheer pleasure rushed through her body with the force of a tidal wave. If he had pulled her to the ground, she would have surrendered to him eagerly.

And then, without warning, a sound jerked them apart as though they were puppets on a string; their hands fell away from each other with the shock of the interruption.

"Dany?" It was Bud, his voice ringing out over the garden. "Dany, there's someone here to see you!" And then, obviously to someone else: "She's probably at the center; I think she likes to sit there."

Another voice reached them. "That sounds like Dany," it commented cheerfully, "communing with nature at all hours. I'll find her, Bud."

Dany stiffened suddenly, recognizing Jason's voice. Oh, no! It would have to be Jason! She turned eyes still sleepy with passion to Bay, an agonizing certainty clamping her heart with icy fingers. And she was right.

His face was a furious mask, his eyes stabbing her with their metallic hardness. "I should have known!" His low voice was shaking with anger. "What was I, you cheating little bitch—a stopgap until your lover arrived?"

"No! Bay, please—"

He shook off the hand she had extended to him, a bitter oath coming from his lips as he flung himself around and strode off toward the far end of the garden.

Dany fastened her blouse with trembling fingers, her shaking legs carrying her only as far as the bench he had been sitting on before she collapsed.

Jason came upon the center of the garden a few moments later, his smile of greeting dying on his lips as he saw the figure huddled on the stone bench. Her face was buried in her hands; wrenching sobs shook her shoulders. Shocked, Jason hurried forward, dropping down beside her on the bench and placing a comforting arm around her shoulders. "Dany! Honey, what's wrong?"

The only answer she gave was to cry even harder, her whole body shaking with the force of some terrible emotion. His face creased with concern, Jason made soothing noises from time to time and let her cry, wondering what had happened to cause her to fall apart like this. He had only seen her lose control so completely once before— when her parents had been killed—and he had no idea what could have happened now to cause her violent grief.

When her sobs had finally trailed away, he thrust his snowy handkerchief into her hands and said quietly, "Tell me what's wrong, Dany."

She dried her eyes and blew her nose, her fingers still trembling as she clutched the scrap of cloth like a lifeline. "It doesn't matter," she said dully. "He'll never believe me now. He doesn't love me. . . . He doesn't trust me. Even if I slept with him to prove there hasn't been anyone else, he'd still hate me. He hates all women."

The flat, disjointed words brought a puzzled frown to

Jason's face. "Who, Dany? Who wouldn't believe you?" he asked, tactfully ignoring the rest of her speech.

"Bay."

"Bay Spencer?" Jason fought to hide his astonishment. "I didn't know you—I thought you couldn't stand the man."

"I can't!" Her voice was suddenly filled with bitter passion. "He's arrogant and hateful, cruel and sarcastic—a savage, heartless *brute*! I hate him!" She buried her face in the handkerchief and burst into tears again, her final statement coming jerky with sobs. "I hate him!"

"I see." Jason really did see; he had been married too long to accept tearfully passionate words at face value. It seemed that cool, aloof Dany had finally tumbled into love—with the one person in the world she had sworn to hate. It would have been funny if it hadn't been so tragic.

He patted her shoulder soothingly, his gray eyes thoughtful as he stared at the hedge-horses in front of them and listened to Dany's broken, emotional words.

"He said . . . that he'd break me . . . but then the bruises seemed to shock him. . . . And he said he wouldn't bother me . . . always with Marissa . . . pricked my finger on the thorn . . . and he was so *gentle!* But then you came. . . . His face . . . He called me a . . . He was so angry. . . ."

Jason sorted out the jumbled fragments as best he could, and waited until her voice faded into silence before saying quietly, "You've had a rough time of it these past few weeks, haven't you?"

Dany blew her nose a final time and stared down at the bunched handkerchief. "Not at first," she said in a low voice. "He was so charming at the beach. We went sailing and walking, and swimming. . . . He treated me like a *person*. I thought he was just a friend. And then, before I realized it . . ."

141

"You fell in love with him," Jason supplied quietly as her voice trailed off.

She nodded jerkily. "I didn't mean for it to happen; I didn't want to love him. But I couldn't fight it. And then you called that night, and—" Her voice broke off abruptly and she stared blindly ahead, her emerald eyes vivid with remembered pain.

Jason shot a swift, narrowed glance at her white face. "I did interrupt something that night."

She nodded again. "Bay was with me. After you called, we had a fight. He said such terrible things! He thought— he *believed*—that you and I were having an affair."

With a sigh Jason murmured, "Those damn rumors."

"Yes. He believes them," she said simply.

"Then that's what you meant about sleeping with him; it's the only way you could convince him of the truth."

The quiet comment brought a faint blush to Dany's cheeks. "I—I have thought about it," she admitted almost inaudibly. "If I thought it would make a difference . . . but it wouldn't. He hates women."

"That doesn't sound like the Spencer I've heard of," Jason said with a startled look at her.

Dany's mouth twisted into a humorless smile. "You're talking about his body; I'm talking about his mind."

The wry comment deepened Jason's frown. Finally he said, "You'll have to explain that."

She fixed her gaze on the hedge-horses. "He—uses women," she responded softly. "The rumors about all the women in his past are probably true; he's very experienced. But it's always a physical thing with him. *Mentally* he—he doesn't like women very much. He seems to expect the very worst from them. I think that he was hurt once—by a woman—and it's twisted something inside of him."

Jason was staring at her with thoughtful eyes. "You've

142

changed, Dany," he said suddenly. "You've grown up." When she turned a startled gaze to him, he smiled slightly. "You've always been so cool, so remote, never seeing beneath the surface of anything. It used to worry me."

Her smile was a little shaky. "It was like there was a curtain between me and the rest of the world, and then Bay came along and—and ripped the curtain away somehow."

"Not completely away," Jason murmured, staring at her intently. "The mask is still there—a little tattered, but still there. And the innocence is still in your eyes."

"If you see innocence in my eyes," she burst out suddenly, "and Darius sees it, and Tony, and Susan—and everyone else, *why can't Bay*? And if he does see it, why doesn't he believe it?"

Slowly, thoughtfully, Jason responded. "Maybe it's true what they say—that love is blind."

"It's certainly turned me into a blind idiot," she said bitterly.

"You're missing the point, honey. Maybe Bay doesn't see the innocence because *he's* blind."

She stared at him, and then shook her head no.

"It's possible, Dany."

"No, you're wrong." Her voice had become jerky again, her gaze fixed on the crumpled handkerchief in her hands. "I—there are things I haven't told you, things I haven't explained. I know he doesn't love me."

Jason remembered her tearful words about bruises and decided that there was probably a great deal she hadn't told him. "Would you like for me to explain to him about this mythical affair of ours?" he asked quietly.

She shook her head quickly, her lips firming stubbornly. "No. Either he believes me or he doesn't; I don't want anyone else trying to convince him."

"You're being pigheaded," Jason told her flatly.

With another shake of her head Dany deliberately changed the subject. "Bud told me that you weren't coming until next week. Why the change of plans?"

"I'm not so sure I should tell you." His voice was expressionless. "You've been through a lot lately; one more shock could be the final straw."

Dany felt a sensation of foreboding creep over her, but she managed to respond calmly. "Tell me. If I keel over, you can always have me carted off to a padded cell."

After a searching look at her face Jason said quietly, "I received a tip from one of my newspaper friends late last night, Dany. There's been a leak."

The foreboding turned to sheer dread. Dry-mouthed, she whispered, "What kind of leak?"

"I think you've already guessed." He sighed heavily. "I'm sorry, honey; the press has found out about your books. They know who Aurora Sanders really is."

Somewhat to her surprise, Dany found that she was not as terrified as she had expected to be. She turned calm eyes to Jason's face. "It's funny . . . but I don't feel anything much. Just a little scared, a little nervous. It's almost—a relief, in a way. No more secrecy."

Jason gazed at her for a long moment. "I was right," he said quietly. "You have grown up. But you'd better be prepared, Dany. There's going to be a lot of flak—and not just from the press. There are some people in modeling and advertising who will go up like supernovas. I don't know who Bud's invited for tonight, but you can bet at least a few of them won't be happy with you."

Dany felt her spirits rise to meet this new challenge, surprised to realize that she did not feel as defeated as she had only moments ago. With an odd little smile she said, "Let's just hope the mask holds out. When does everything hit the fan, Jason?"

"New Yorkers are reading about it right now with their

morning coffee," he told her wryly. "The rest of the world won't be far behind. There will be a lot of speculation, since you haven't made a statement, but the bare facts are there."

Dany's smile widened to one of sheer amusement. "Why didn't you call me from New York instead of rushing out here?"

"Are you kidding?" He grinned faintly. "As soon as I got the news I booked the first flight I could get. You aren't the only one who's going to get hit with the flak! I have quite a few friends in the fashion world. It didn't bother them to think that *A Time for Serena* was just a novel; when they find out who wrote it, there will be a loud clamoring for my hide to be nailed to the barn door!"

She laughed softly. "Here I was thinking that you'd come out here to protect me, and now I find that I'm supposed to be *your* shield."

He chuckled in response. "Not quite that. I just decided that we might as well stick together."

Dany smiled at him, and then glanced toward the main part of the house, her eyes thoughtful. "Does Bud get any of the New York papers? I haven't noticed."

Jason shook his head. "This is his retreat; he only had the phone put in because his wife insisted. The news probably won't get here until the guests arrive."

She sighed. "Tony's been very kind to me; I'd better warn him. I suppose we should tell Bud too. But no one else, Jason! The rest of them don't have to know yet."

"What about Spencer?"

Dany's lips firmed again in that stubborn expression. "Especially not him."

Jason started to argue with her, but changed his mind. "Okay. I guess you know what you're doing."

Dany only wished that she did. With a smile that hid

her inner uncertainty she said, "Why don't we go and have breakfast? I'm starving."

Jason accompanied her to the lodge, glad that she had apparently thrown off her depression. But he couldn't help wondering exactly what had happened between her and Bay—and how the producer would react to the news of Dany's book.

Only one thing happened to disturb Dany's grimly held peace during that day and, oddly enough, it was an observation of Jason's. For once, all the guests had lunch at the same time, and afterward it seemed natural for them to go into the great room. They automatically formed small groups, as people tended to do when gathered together, and the room was so large that no one in one group could hear the conversation going on in another.

Bud, Cy, Susan, and Tony sat together near the archway to the dining room; Dany, Jason, and Darius occupied chairs near the archway nearest to the bedrooms; and Bay and Marissa were seated before the fireplace.

Dany was trying desperately to forget that Marissa was perched on the arm of Bay's chair and whispering into his ear, but she couldn't help glancing that way from time to time. Her eyes never met Bay's, but she was conscious of his gaze on her more than once.

Her attention was suddenly riveted on her two companions, however, when they began a casual discussion between themselves which sounded almost as though it had been rehearsed.

"It's funny how those two look at each other," Darius remarked, staring fixedly at his thumbnail.

"It certainly is," Jason agreed. "He looks at her when she's looking somewhere else, and she looks at him when he's looking somewhere else."

"And they both have the same expression in their eyes,"

Darius said almost absently, studying the well-pared nail as though it held all the secrets of the universe.

Jason began to contemplate his own thumb. "If their eyes would meet just once . . ." he murmured.

". . . the room would go up in flames," Darius continued with suspicious smoothness.

Dany glared at them both. "I suppose you both think you're being very subtle," she accused irritably.

Jason looked at Darius with an expression of pained surprise on his face. "Were you trying to be subtle?"

Darius shrugged. "I wouldn't recognize subtlety if it bit me on the nose. I was just stating a fact."

"So was I." Jason turned his eyes to Dany. "We were just stating a fact," he told her gravely.

Dany looked even more irritated. "You're both imagining things," she said flatly.

"Are we?" Darius raised his eyes to look at her levelly.

"Yes." Dany avoided his intent gaze.

Softly Jason said, "He looks at you like a starving man eyeing a banquet."

Dany's breath caught in her throat; she lowered her eyes hastily to her tightly clasped hands. "You're wrong."

"And you look at him the same way," Darius said with calm conviction.

Bitterly Dany said, "I should have expected something like this when I found out that you two were old friends; it isn't fair to gang up on me!"

Jason sighed, giving up the pretense. "We're just trying to pound some sense into you, honey. I don't know what these walls are that you two have managed to build between you, but one of you has to start tearing them down."

"I can't," she said intensely, without raising her eyes. "I don't know how!"

"Tell him how you feel," Darius counselled.

"Oh, no!" Dany shook her head quickly. "That would just give him another weapon to use against me."

"*Another* weapon?" Jason looked puzzled.

Dany felt a blush creeping up her cheeks as she remembered her reaction to Bay's touch. "I'd rather not talk about it," she muttered uncomfortably.

Darius returned his attention to his thumbnail. "The way they look at each other," he murmured. "Flames."

Jason's puzzled expression vanished. "Oh." He stared at his young friend. "Well, never mind that. Bay isn't the only one with walls, you know. You've got a hell of a wall yourself." He waited until she raised her eyes, then said, "And that wall of yours isn't exactly tumbling down."

She frowned slightly. "Well, it certainly doesn't seem to be doing me much good. It didn't take you two long to figure out how I feel."

Jason made an impatient gesture. "Your eyes have always shown emotion, Dany," he said flatly. "It's your thoughts the mask hides. That's why you're such a famous model: the emotions are there, but the thoughts behind them are hidden." He shook his head wryly. "It's worse than Mona Lisa's smile."

Dany grinned faintly at the comparison but shook her head as she got to her feet. "It wouldn't work," she said quietly. "Even if all the walls came tumbling down . . . it still wouldn't work. There's been too much bitterness." She hesitated, then murmured, "I'll spend the afternoon in my room, I think. I didn't get much sleep last night. See you two at dinner."

Leaving her concerned friends in the great room, she went down the hall to her bedroom, wishing that they were right about the way Bay looked at her, but knowing in her heart that they were wrong.

Dany dressed carefully that evening, knowing that she

148

would need all the confidence she could get. Her afternoon nap had helped, though she had awakened to the realization that her dreams had not been happy ones, and her face was not quite as pale as it had been that morning.

Tony had received the news of her authorship with his usual calm, unperturbed by her warning that tonight's guests would not be a happy lot. He had simply presented her with another of his lovely creations, telling her that it had been designed to be worn on a special occasion.

Staring at her reflected image in the full-length mirror in her bathroom, Dany sent another mental salute to Tony's genius. The gown was made of delicate silk—so delicate, in fact, that it was impossible to wear anything underneath it—and fell in a shimmering fall of golden fire to her feet. It was magnificent.

Like the seductive green gown she had worn that first night, this one also appeared to cling to her slender body as if it had a mind of its own, and Dany didn't worry this time that it would suddenly decide to leave her. She felt amazingly confident in the gown.

She heard the excited buzz of conversation long before she reached the great room, and she paused for a moment outside the archway to gather her courage. Then, with a faint, cool smile on her face, she stepped into the room.

CHAPTER NINE

Almost immediately silence swept the room, and Dany's courage nearly deserted her. But then Jason and Darius came forward to meet her, their reassuring smiles making her feel secure again. Darius handed her a glass of sherry with a murmured compliment, and Jason took up a position at her side, obviously determined to stand by her through what was to come. They didn't have long to wait.

"Dany!" It was Marissa, of course, coming toward them in a cloud of pink chiffon. "Darling, there's some absurd rumor flying round New York that you wrote that book everyone's talking about!" She gave a light, artificial laugh, her blue eyes very sharp. "I told everyone that it just wasn't possible our quiet little Dany could have written such a vicious book, but they don't seem to believe me."

As usual, Marissa had managed to draw attention to herself, but that was short-lived. All eyes swung at once to Dany's faintly smiling face, more than a little curious to discover her reaction to the blonde's malicious remarks.

Still smiling, Dany asked casually, "Have you read the book, Marissa?"

"Oh, darling, you know I never read novels!"

"You should read this one." Dany smiled very gently. "You're in it."

Marissa's smile faltered just a little. "How would you know that, Dany?" she asked sweetly.

"Because I put you there." Dany sipped her drink calmly, an unusual glitter in the green eyes. "You're Kate."

Marissa didn't have to read the novel to find out that the character of Kate was not a particularly nice one; the smothered laughter she heard from some of the guests who *had* read the book told her that. Both her smile and her blue eyes were sheathed in ice as she stared at Dany. Making a mental note to get even with her rival, she asked, "Then you did write the book?"

Dany glanced around the room, seeing hostility on some of the watching faces and simple curiosity on others. Her eyes fell at last on Bay's face, and she felt the tiny hope within her shrivel beneath the arctic coldness of his stare. The glitter in her own eyes died; she felt her courage falter. Then, lifting her chin slightly, she met Bay's metallic gaze expressionlessly. "Yes. I wrote *A Time for Serena* . . . and the other three novels attributed to Aurora Sanders."

After that quiet announcement the evening turned into one of the worst ordeals of Dany's life. Not all of the guests were upset about the novel—only those who saw themselves or their friends fictionalized in a book written by a model. Even then they might have been willing to forgive Dany if she had insisted that the book was merely a novel, but she didn't. She told them, quite honestly, that her book was more or less autobiographical, and that she would make that statement to the press as soon as she returned to New York.

152

Needless to say, that set the seal on the wave of hostility aimed toward her, and it took every ounce of Dany's self-control to get through the remainder of the evening. Aided whenever possible by Jason and Darius, she dealt quietly with probing questions and veiled threats of blacklisting, and tried to ignore the icy blue eyes of the man who watched her with steellike anger. Bay was drinking more than usual, and his eyes never once left Dany's face. His fixed stare was so intense that everyone in the room soon became aware of it—which gave them something else to speculate about.

It only added to Dany's problems. His brooding anger frightened her; it was oddly unlike him to make his emotions so blatantly obvious to all. And Marissa, at first pleased by the hostility directed at her rival, soon became enraged by the fact that Bay was ignoring everyone but Dany. She tried in every way she knew to capture his attention, but when he told her in a curt, hard voice to leave him alone—without mincing words—her rage knew no bounds.

So Dany was forced to endure Marissa's vicious tongue as well as the rest, and by the time everyone returned to the great room after dinner, she was a quivering mass of nerves. Her thoughts were hidden from prying eyes as effectively as they had ever been, but her lovely face became more and more strained as the evening wore on. By ten o'clock she could bear it no longer, and quietly excused herself to Jason and Darius. Both of them encouraged her to get some rest, and she nodded tiredly before leaving the room.

Dany felt too upset to rest, however. She paused in her room only long enough to exchange her high-heeled sandals for a pair of slide-ons, and then opened her patio door and went out into the silent moonlit garden. Holding the skirt of her golden gown to keep it from dragging on the ground, she made her way along a graveled path until she came to a secluded spot that she had discovered some days before. It was on the outer edges of the garden, a small section that had been allowed to grow wild.

Automatically holding her skirt high, Dany stepped through the tangled profusion of rosebushes and then sat down on the old iron bench that was invisible from any of the paths. She felt the need to be alone with her thoughts, and this was the most private place she knew.

She sat in silence, her hands clasped together loosely in her lap, listening to the soft night sounds and inhaling the heavy yet oddly delicate scent of the roses. The garden gave her no peace this time—but then she had not really expected it to. She felt so tired, drained of everything except confusion.

The worry over her book was a fleeting thing; it had not even been able to hold her full attention for more than a few minutes at a time during the evening. Bay had done that. Not a moment had passed without her awareness of his presence, his nearness. She had wanted to cross the room and beg him to tell her why he was so angry. She had wanted to throw herself into his arms and surrender mindlessly to the need that was tearing her apart. Only his anger and her own pride had kept her from doing just that.

Why go on deceiving herself? She belonged to him. He had made her his the very first time he had held her in his arms, and she belonged to him. By his demand? By her own choice? No. By something more powerful than either of them, something so elemental, so primitive, that it had no name. It was as if she had been formed, shaped, only to join with him. In his arms she felt alive, complete. Apart from him she was only a shell filled with restless hunger.

With a shaking sigh Dany dropped her head in her hands and tried to think. Could she return to New York—

or her beach house—and pick up the threads of her life? Was she strong enough to face the future, knowing that Bay would not be a part of it? Did she have a choice?

God—what a question! Of course, she had a choice. She could accept Bay on his own terms, give herself to him on a purely physical basis; or she could run like a thief and hide somewhere, comforted by the knowledge that she still had her self-respect. Hide! she thought bitterly. What use would that be? If she never saw Bay again, his image would live on forever in her heart.

In any case, she acknowledged tiredly, he probably didn't even want her anymore. The look in his eyes tonight had not been one of desire; it had been an expression of sheer fury. She didn't understand that anger. She didn't understand his mental dislike of women. And she didn't know how to fight either one.

Wearily Dany pushed the questions from her mind. It was a long time later when she finally rose to her feet and started back toward her bedroom. When she passed the main section of the lodge, she was vaguely surprised to see that the great room was darkened; obviously she had spent more time in the garden than she had realized.

She stepped into her bedroom, lighted only by the lamp that she had left burning, and immediately halted, her eyes drawn to the leanly dangerous form rising from the chair beside her bed. She slid the patio door closed with nerveless fingers and had to swallow twice before words would emerge. "What are you doing here?"

"Waiting for you." His voice grated harshly on her ears, his metallic eyes stabbing her across the width of the room. "Where have you been, Dany? With Carrington? Sneaking through the garden so no one would know?"

Dany flinched only slightly, half expecting him to make some sort of accusation. Too drained to feel even anger, she said dully, "I was in the garden. Alone."

155

He laughed tauntingly. "I'll just bet you were! Did you tell him about this morning, Dany? Did you tell him what he interrupted? Or doesn't he care?"

"Why won't you believe me?" she burst out tremulously. "Jason isn't my lover! He's my friend and my publisher —nothing more!"

"Dammit, I don't care anymore," he muttered suddenly, crossing the space between them in two quick strides. His fingers bit into her shoulders as he stared down at her. "You've been handing out your favors to everyone else—I hope you've saved something for me!"

Dany barely had time to grasp the significance of the sudden flame in his eyes, before his dark head swooped, the firm lips capturing hers with ruthless intensity. His kiss was a savage brand, and Dany, her lips having parted to form a protest, was helpless to prevent her instant response. Her conscious mind was submerged beneath a wave of desire so powerful that it left her reeling. His mouth took hers violently, with none of the morning's gentleness, the sensuous probing of his tongue sending an invading weakness through her limbs.

Dany's arms slid up around his neck, her mouth opened willingly beneath his, and immediately the anger seemed to drain away from him. The hard lips gentled; his hand slid down her back to her hips, pulling her yielding body firmly against the strength of his. She felt his hardening thighs pulsing with desire, and a responding ache began to form in her loins.

His lips left hers to explore the hollows of her throat, searing wherever they touched, trailing fire in a hungry path across her soft skin. "Oh, God, I want you," he muttered, his teeth tugging gently at the lobe of her ear.

Mindless, robbed of all will, Dany locked her fingers in the soft thickness of his black hair, pulling his mouth back

156

to hers with helpless need. All that mattered to her was the satisfaction of this terrible soul-destroying hunger.

There was a whisper of sound, and she felt a sudden coolness against her heated flesh as the dress fell to the floor in a shower of gold. Her arms around his neck, her fingers exploring the corded strength of his shoulders through the thin silk shirt, she made no protest when he swept her into his arms and carried her to the bed.

He lowered her there, his body half covering hers, their lips still fused together. Dany coped feverishly with the buttons of his shirt, pushing it off his shoulders and only half aware of him throwing it to the floor. He lifted his lips from hers, turning his indigo gaze to the naked splendor of her slim white body. "You're so lovely," he said hoarsely, his burning eyes playing over the tempting curves.

Green eyes clouded with passion, Dany watched his absorbed face, vaguely surprised to feel no shame or embarrassment to have this man see her as no other had done before. She was suddenly conscious of a fierce gladness at the knowledge that he found her beautiful, and when his mouth lowered to capture the tip of one rosy breast, her body arched against him of its own will, a moan breaking from her lips.

Dizzying sensations flooded her body, her breath came rapidly in shallow pants as his hands and lips caressed, finding all the secret places of pleasure. The ache in her loins grew steadily, an empty agony, until she could bear it no longer. Moving restlessly beneath him, her nails digging into his back, she whispered raggedly, "Please . . . oh, God—please!"

He took one of her hands and placed it on the waistband of his pants. "What, Dany? Tell me what you want," he commanded.

Shock poured icy water over the fire in Dany's veins as

she heard the note of implacable certainty in his voice. Her desire fled as quickly as it had come, leaving only a cold, aching emptiness within her. Her hands slowly fell away from him, painful tears rising in her eyes, too numb even to feel the erotic lips on her breast. In a husky whisper she said, "I don't know who she was—the woman who hurt you so badly—but I don't want to be punished for her mistakes."

He stiffened, his head lifting as he stared down into the tear-bright emerald eyes. A spasm of pain crossed his face, and he rolled away from her, sitting up on the edge of the bed and raking unsteady hands through his hair. "My mother," he bit out savagely.

Dany stared at the broad, tense back, her breath catching in her throat at the bitterness in his voice. "Your mother?"

He nodded jerkily, keeping his back to her. "My father was a producer. Whenever he was on location, my mother and I would remain at home. He'd been in Europe for several weeks when I came home from school early one day. My—she was in the living room with some actor."

"How old were you?" Dany whispered.

"Twelve." He laughed harshly. "Old enough to know damn well what was going on."

"You could have been wrong about—"

"I wasn't wrong! That bastard was just one of many. After I'd seen her that day, she didn't bother to hide it. They came and went whenever my father was away."

Dany listened silently to the pent-up memories, compassion stirring within her as she heard the pain of the child's betrayal quivering in the man's voice.

"She was so beautiful, so charming. She had only to smile, and people bent over backward for her. My father worshiped her!"

Silently Dany thought that her son had worshiped her,

158

too, and she understood now why he was so bitter. What a terrible shock for a twelve-year-old boy to see his mother tumble off the pedestal on which he had lovingly placed her!

"It destroyed my father when he found out about the other men. Oh, I didn't tell him," Bay went on, as if he had picked up Dany's silent question. "My father found out about it the same way I had; he came home unexpectedly and caught her."

"Did they stay together?"

"They lived together," he answered flatly. "I'd lie in bed at night and hear them fighting, tearing each other to bits. My father started drinking, neglecting his work. He was a brilliant man—a legend in the film industry—and for four years I watched him fall apart!"

"And—and after that?"

"I went away to school, never saw them again. They were killed in a plane crash on their way to visit me at college."

"All these years you've hated women because of what your mother did," Dany whispered, staring at him. His shoulders moved, rejecting the idea, and her hand reached to touch the tanned flesh of his back. "Bay, I'm sorry, but—"

He jerked as though her hand had been a live wire. "Damn you!" he flung over one shoulder. "I don't want your sympathy!"

"Then what do you want?" Her voice was torn with emotion. "How can I convince you that all women aren't like your mother was?"

"You can't!" He laughed harshly. "All women are alike. Heartless, grasping little bitches, every last one! Selling their bodies for a part in a film, or an introduction to someone important—God, do you think I don't know?"

Dany remembered the rumors about him, all the

women who had thrown themselves at his feet, the actresses who had become famous in his films, and thought that he probably had good reason to feel the way he did. Very quietly, she said, "All women aren't alike."

"They are!" A muscle jumped violently in his jaw; he didn't look at her. "I thought you were different. Damn you, I thought you weren't like the rest! But you are. You've got Carrington and Tremaine dangling on a string —both of them powerful, wealthy men. You've lied about that damn book—"

"I didn't!" she interrupted desperately. "I never lied about the book. I kept that secret for five years; no one was supposed to find out until my contract at the agency ran out. That's why Jason came here; he wanted to warn me that the press had gotten hold of the story."

"He came here to be with you," Bay said grimly. "Do you think I didn't see the way he hovered over you all evening—him and Tremaine?"

Dany pressed one hand against her stomach, feeling it grow taut with nervous tension. She was completely unconscious of her nudity, frantically trying to think of some way to convince him she was telling the truth. With a ring of bitterness in her voice she said, "What do you want me to do, Bay—sleep with you to prove there's been no man in my life?"

"That wouldn't prove anything," he said with harsh cruelty.

"Yes, it would," she said quietly.

He stiffened suddenly, shooting a quick glance over his shoulder at her shadowed face. "What's that supposed to mean?" he asked tightly.

"There's been no man in my life, Bay. *No* man."

"You're not a virgin, Dany," he said flatly. "You can't be; you've been a model too long."

With a deep breath Dany burned all her bridges behind her. "I know of only one way to prove it to you."

Every muscle in his body seemed to tighten suddenly. "What now, Dany? Are you going to offer yourself to me to prove you're a virgin?" His voice was raspy.

"If that's what it takes to convince you," she said levelly.

There was a long silence, and then he rose and bent to pick up his shirt from the floor. "Damn you," he muttered, shrugging into the shirt. "I can't take you now, and you know it. If it turned out you'd been telling the truth, I'd feel guilty as hell!"

He strode to the door and then halted, one hand on the knob. As if compelled by something beyond his power to fight, he turned and gazed across the room at the slender girl lying so still on the bed. The soft light from the lamp on the nightstand cast a warm glow over her bare body, painting shadows and highlights with a lover's hand.

Bay's face tightened, a tormented expression shining in his eyes for a brief moment. And then he turned back to the door, wrenching it open and slamming it behind him as he left the room.

After a moment Dany rose from the bed and crossed to the dresser. She did not look at her reflected body, but stared instead at her face. Even in the faint glow from the lamp, she saw what Bay had missed. His vulnerability had accomplished what his strength and determination could not: The mask was gone.

Dany walked in the garden early the next afternoon, unable to face anyone. She had spent the morning at the stables, and had sneaked (what a horrible word!) into the kitchen to make herself a sandwich around noon. Mrs. Collins, the housekeeper, had not seemed upset that one of the guests had invaded her domain, but had talked to

161

Dany in a garrulous manner that had finally driven her out into the garden.

Thoughts of the night before haunted her, filling her with painful shame. Bay had rejected her—again. And even though she understood his reasons for doing so, it did not make the rejection any easier to bear. Even as she had offered herself to him, she had known that the mask was gone, had known that if he had looked into her eyes, he would have seen the love she was no longer capable of hiding. It hadn't mattered to her. Moved by his emotional confession—his bitter denouncement of all women as promiscuous creatures—she had wanted only to prove that she, at least, was different.

But now she wondered miserably if she hadn't proved the opposite. He had not seen the helpless love in her eyes, and to him it had probably seemed as though she had offered herself to him only cold-bloodedly to prove a point. Even though he had not believed her claim of virginity, his innate decency had prevented him from taking advantage of her offer, and she could only be grateful for that small mercy.

What had he thought? she wondered, her cheeks burning with shame. She had told him that she hated him, and yet she had been unable to fight her body's response to his passion. She had offered herself without making him understand that her desire had its roots in love. And, in doing so, she had only intensified his contempt of her. She must have seemed like a tease! Capitulating verbally yet making it impossible for him to possess her because of her assertion of virginity.

God, what a fool she was! It had simply not occurred to her that Bay would feel guilty after taking her virginity. And, she remembered suddenly, there had been no emotion in her voice as she had offered herself—as if she had nerved herself to make some noble sacrifice, for God's sake!

He didn't know that she had abandoned her pride at that moment, didn't know that her heart had been racing like a runaway train. He only knew that she had made a cold, emotionless offer of her body to prove a point.

With no awareness of where her wanderings had led her, Dany sank down on the stone bench in front of the hedge-horses and stared blindly at nothing.

"I thought I'd find you here!"

She looked up quickly, her heartbeat returning to normal when she saw Bud coming toward her.

He sat down on the bench beside her. "I'm glad I found you alone; I want to talk to you, Dany."

"What about?" She fixed her eyes on the hedge-horses.

"Bay's like a grizzly with a sore head," he said lightly. "What have you been doing to him, Dany?"

She felt her stomach tighten suddenly, but managed a faint smile. "It's the other way around," she murmured.

"Oh. What's he been doing to you?"

She flushed. "Can't I have any secrets?"

"You're under my roof, Dany. I invited you here—at Bay's request—and I feel responsible for you." He hesitated. "Bay told me that he wanted to spend some time with you informally, to talk to you about taking a part in his new film. But after seeing the two of you together . . . Dany, do you mind a little fatherly advice?"

She laughed involuntarily, half rueful, half tearful. "I have three pseudofathers here, and the other two have offered their advice. It's your turn, I guess."

After a moment he said quietly, "Bay's a complicated man. Like an iceberg, most of him is beneath the surface. I've known him all his life, and I know what I'm talking about. To understand him you have to understand some-

163

thing that happened to him when he was a child. His mother—"

"I know," she interrupted flatly. "He told me about his mother."

Bud seemed oddly satisfied by her remark. "Did he? I thought maybe he had. Well, let me tell you something more about that. Bay adored Rebecca, idolized her. He probably wouldn't admit it now, but it was from her that he inherited most of his strength and determination. Richard was a creative genius, a brilliant man, but he wasn't strong. He never would have become so successful if it hadn't been for her. Rebecca had all the ambition that he lacked. She had grown up in grinding poverty, and it had left her with a hunger for money and power.

"She was playing a bit part in a third-rate film when she met Richard, and she was intelligent enough to realize that he had the potential to become great in the industry. Richard fell in love with her immediately, and they were married within a week."

Bud sighed, his gray eyes looking more than thirty-five years into the past. "Rebecca played all the Hollywood games as if she had invented them herself. She spared no effort to get Richard noticed and talked about. She found backers for his films, pored over scripts. She dragged him to all the glamorous parties he hated, angling for introductions to all the right people. She made him a success.

"Richard adored her. To him she was the most perfect woman in the world and—like most dreamers—he was completely blind to anything negative. He let her manage his career because it made her happy. When she became pregnant, he was delighted. He never realized that she was not a maternal woman, never saw her resentment. Her pregnancy kept her out of circulation for nearly a year, and when she tried to rejoin the society that she loved, it was to discover that she had been forgotten."

Dany looked startled, and Bud shrugged slightly. "Hollywood has a short memory. She found that she was only the wife of Richard Spencer, and though that gave her a certain amount of power, it wasn't enough for her. I guess it turned her bitter after a time; the spotlight that *she* had focused on Richard was no longer wide enough to include her. Richard's talent had become known by then, and he no longer needed her to manage his career. He wanted her and his child to have a secure, stable life, so he left them at home and went on location alone."

"If she was so cold and—and resentful," Dany said slowly, "how was it that Bay didn't feel her lack of love for him?"

Bud shrugged again. "Who can truly understand the workings of a child's mind, Dany? With his father's lead to follow, he just worshiped her with blind devotion. Neither one of them realized how bitter she was, how much she hated being on the sidelines of Richard's fame."

"And—the other men?"

"That started when Bay was about ten," Bud murmured with a faint sigh. "Richard was spending more and more time away from home, and Rebecca . . . well, her beauty was fading, and the admiration of her husband and child just wasn't enough for her. She turned to other men."

"Bay said . . . it destroyed his father."

"It did," Bud said flatly. "Richard was never the same after he found out about Rebecca's affairs. He started drinking; there were bitter—often public—fights between them. Rebecca was sick, Dany; she needed admiration like an addict needs a fix. By the time Richard realized that—if he ever did—it was too late. The damage had been done."

Dany stared down at her clasped hands. "And Bay never recovered from the shock of finding out what his mother was."

Very quietly Bud said, "It put a crust on him, Dany. His illusions about his mother were shattered with one blow, and it only made it worse for him to watch his father suffering as only a romantic *can* suffer. After his parents were killed, Bay went on to become even more famous than his father had been, and he grew cynical. Everything was too easy for him; he never had to fight. He's always believed that women wanted him because of what he could give them, and never for himself alone. He's never known real love, Dany."

"Why have you told me all this?" she asked, continuing to stare blindly at her hands.

"There's been a lot of bedroom doors slamming around here lately," Bud responded gently. "And I've watched Bay go through more honest emotions than he has in his life. You've shaken him off his balance, Dany. Somehow, you've managed to touch a nerve inside him. He inherited a romantic nature from his father, and it's been encased in ice all these years. But that ice is cracking now. Because of you."

"Marissa . . ." Dany murmured, afraid to believe what Bud was telling her.

"He doesn't pace the floor at night because of Marissa," Bud told her softly. "He doesn't watch her when she isn't watching him. And when she's not in the room, he doesn't look up every time someone comes in hoping it'll be her."

Still afraid to hope, Dany said, "He doesn't trust me. He gets so angry sometimes. . . ."

"He's never learned to trust, Dany. And, as for the anger—a man in the final throes of admitting to love is often angry. Especially when he doesn't believe in the emotion torturing him. And it is torturing him, Dany." After a moment Bud said gently, "Can't you put him out of his misery? Can't you tell him that you love him?"

Dany lifted tear-bright emerald eyes to him, her face

166

pale. "It wouldn't do any good," she whispered. "Something happened. . . . I made him think that I—that I'm just like the women he's known. I made him think—oh, God! I've made such a mess of things!"

Bud's hand came out to cover the ones tightly clenched in her lap. "It's not too late, Dany. Don't let a misunderstanding keep you two apart! He loves you—whether he knows it or not. For the first time in his life, he's reaching out to someone. *Be there,* Dany! Convince him that love is a strength and not a weakness. Show him that he doesn't have to be afraid to love."

Dany stared straight ahead for a long moment, her mind whirling with the things he had told her. What if he was wrong? Could she take the chance? One more rejection from the man she loved would destroy her, she knew. She remembered Jason and Darius both advising her to tell Bay how she felt. And now Bud. But none of them knew exactly what had gone on between her and Bay. None of them had heard the harsh words or felt the bitter pain that she had felt.

With an abrupt movement she rose to her feet. "I have to think. I have to be alone for a while," she murmured.

"He'll die without you, Dany," Bud said very quietly.

Bay? Strong, ruthless Bay? It seemed—it was!—impossible. He couldn't feel so deeply about her! She made a helpless little gesture. "I have to think," she repeated. "I—I'll see you later, Bud." Without waiting for a response, Dany began to make her way through the garden, her feet turning instinctively toward the stables. She had to get away—completely away—from the lodge.

It didn't take long to saddle a horse. The trainer, who had enjoyed a casual talk with her only that morning, was glad to perform the service for her. She chose as her mount a pure bred Arabian mare who was, according to the trainer, skittish in a storm, but otherwise perfectly behaved. He told her chattily as he saddled the horse that there were numerous trails she could follow. In particular, he advised, there was the trail by the stream, which ended near a small cabin.

Only half hearing him, Dany responded politely to the advice, acknowledged his remark that the mare was named Ladama with an absent nod, and mounted without his assistance. Within moments she was following one of the trails that he had pointed out, and soon the trees hid the lodge from sight.

Dany lost track of time as she rode. She had learned to ride almost as early as she had learned to walk, and so needed little of her concentration to remain in the saddle. She gave the mare her head, not particularly caring where she went, too disturbed to notice that the sky was slowly gathering the leaden appearance of an approaching storm.

Bud's talk with her had only added to her confusion; she was still afraid to hope that Bay could love as well as desire her. She wanted to believe it. Oh, God, yes—she wanted desperately to believe it! But her quivering heart had taken too many blows to be able to contemplate the possibility of yet another without flinching.

"He'll die without you, Dany."

The words went round and round in her head, tormenting her with the image they painted, driving every other thought from her mind. She rode for hours.

Some instinct warned her quite suddenly that all was not right, and she looked up through a break in the trees to see frowning dark clouds. The wind rustled through the trees with new strength, and Dany shivered as it made itself felt through her thin cotton shirt. Aware now of her mount's nervousness, she made up her mind to return to the lodge, when a rabbit burst suddenly from the undergrowth and darted across the rocky path directly in front of the horse.

With a scream of fear, the scent of the hated storm in her nostrils, Ladama reared. Sheer instinct kept Dany in the saddle; she tried to bring the mare's head around, knowing that the animal would bolt in terror the instant her front hooves touched the ground. But instead of lunging forward, Ladama scarcely waited to get all four hooves on the ground before shying violently and whirling back the way they had come.

Caught off guard and off balance, Dany felt herself falling, and had just enough presence of mind to kick her feet free of the stirrups. She landed badly, feeling a wrenching pain as her ankle twisted beneath her; then her head struck a rock on the path, and darkness closed over her.

CHAPTER TEN

The woods were dark and ominously silent when Dany regained consciousness. Feeling dizzy and sick, she made no attempt to stir from her lying position, but raised one hand to press against her throbbing right temple. The hand came away sticky with blood, and for a moment she had to fight the instinctive panic that the sight of one's own blood often brings. Then, taking a calming breath, she forced herself to examine her temple with shaking fingers. A sigh of relief escaped her as she realized that it was only a small cut, bleeding alarmingly as scalp wounds tended to do.

Her relief made her reckless; she sat up faster than she should have, and was immediately punished as pain shot up her left leg. The ankle she had landed on was swelled to twice its normal size and hot to the touch. Only the discovery that she could move her foot—albeit painfully —reassured her that the ankle was not broken. Gritting her teeth against the pain, she somehow managed to pull herself up, hanging on to a tree and carefully keeping her weight off the injured ankle.

Fighting off the attack of dizziness that her upright position had brought, she stared around until she saw the broken branches and churned-up earth that were mute evidence of the mare's terrified flight. Experience with horses told her that Ladama would not stop running until she reached the security of her stable, and common sense told her that she herself could not make it back to the lodge without help.

Listening intently, she could just barely hear the distant sound of running water, and she suddenly remembered the trainer mentioning the trail by the stream and a hunter's cabin. But where was it? The faint sound of water seemed to come from every direction. Memories of childhood lessons in woodsmanship came to her rescue, and with her teeth clamped tightly to keep back the cries of pain, she left the path and began to hobble downhill. It took more than half an hour to locate the stream, and Dany's strength was exhausted by the time she found it.

A lovely, picturesque scene met her weary eyes as she emerged from the woods and into the uncertain sunshine. Clear water gurgled merrily between flower-lined banks and splashed down a small waterfall directly in front of her. The waterfall drew Dany like a magnet, and she carefully lowered herself onto a large boulder beside it. Slowly she extended her injured ankle until it was beneath the waterfall, shoe and all. Blessed coolness flowed over the throbbing ankle, and Dany sat perfectly still for a long moment, her tensed muscles slowly relaxing.

After a while she wet the tail of her shirt and rather gingerly cleaned the bruised skin around the cut on her temple. The wound had finally stopped bleeding, and though it throbbed in concert with her ankle, her vision was clear, and the dizziness had gone. No concussion, she thought with relief, and then glanced up as dark clouds blotted out the weak sunshine.

That one glance made her draw her ankle from the water with cautious haste and drag herself back into the woods. She searched for ten minutes before she found the path, and then flipped a mental coin to decide which way to go. The path wound beside the stream fairly constantly, and Dany's arbitrary decision took her upstream rather than down—a choice she hoped would eventually lead to the old cabin that the trainer had spoken of. Judging by the heavy sky, she knew a storm was rapidly approaching, and she did not want to be caught without shelter.

The journey would live long in Dany's mind as being the worst of her life. She had found a stick strong enough for her to lean on, but it didn't stop the pain that shot up her leg at every step, and the rocky path made going even more difficult. By the time the small cabin came into view, she was sobbing with pain and exhaustion, and the sight was more welcome than a palace.

A tiny corral and three-sided shed flanked the cabin, taking up the remainder of the small clearing. Everything seemed sturdy and in good repair, doubtless made use of often during the hunting season.

Leaning heavily on her stick, Dany limped across to the door and pushed it open. To her relief the interior of the structure, though dark and musty-smelling, was relatively clean. The light pouring through the open door showed a stone fireplace at the opposite wall, a wooden table to the right of the fireplace and toward the center of the room, and a wooden bench and ladder-back chair on either side of the table.

Dany glanced around warily for any sign of furry inhabitants and, seeing none, dragged herself into the room. She left the door open and, by its light, was able to locate a soot-covered lantern. Further search revealed a box of kitchen matches on a wooden shelf above a plentiful supply of firewood stacked in one corner of the cabin, and she silently thanked the Fates for both.

Half an hour later, a warm and comforting fire blazed in the stone fireplace, and the sooty lamp provided a faint glow. With a sigh Dany set the lamp on one end of the table and then hobbled to the other end and sank down wearily in the sturdy chair. She leaned forward for a moment to throw another log on the fire, feeling a damp chill in the air and knowing that the storm clouds she had seen had not been one of nature's idle boasts. She moved the chair slightly so that she could rest an elbow on the table, keeping her back to the fire and her eyes on the door.

Time passed slowly; the grimy window by the door grew dark, as night and the storm approached. Having no idea of how far she had ridden, Dany wondered tiredly whether or not Ladama had returned to the stables and if a search party had been formed. She leaned her head back against the chair, closing her eyes as she listened to the wind's whisper rise to a howl. Like Ladama, she had always possessed an irrational fear of storms, and her nails bit into her palms as she heard the first faint rumble of thunder in the distance. Rain began to patter softly and steadily on the tin roof.

When he came, it was with the silence of some night creature. He pushed open the door and stood on the threshold, the firelight glinting off the wet black slicker shrouding his lean form as his hard gaze swept the room. The taut face relaxed somewhat as he saw her sitting by the table. He stared at her shadowy face for a moment. "Are you all right?" he asked in a brusque voice.

Strangely unsurprised to see him, Dany nodded slowly. "Yes. I'm fine."

"I'll signal the others." Without another word he turned and went back outside. It was too dark to see anything, but Dany heard him speak—apparently to his

174

horse—and a moment later there came the sharp crack of a rifle. Half expecting the sound, Dany nonetheless jumped, and bit back a moan as her head and ankle throbbed in protest. She barely heard the distant answering shot.

Bay came in just then, propping his rifle beside the door and crossing to drop a sleeping bag on the floor in front of the fire. Saddlebags were slung over his shoulder, and as he turned to place them on the table, he saw the rapidly darkening bruise surrounding the cut on her temple. "What the hell?"

"I'm fine," she said flatly. "I hit my head when I fell, that's all."

"You could have a concussion," he responded grimly.

"I don't have a concussion. I've been concussed before, and I remember very well what it felt like."

He rummaged in one of the saddlebags and produced a first-aid kit, then dropped the bags on the bench across from her. Placing the first-aid kit on the table, he reached out a hand to touch her cheek. "That's a nasty cut."

Involuntarily she flinched, nervously aware of her body's betraying response to his nearness, his touch. She wanted to fling herself into his arms, but memory of their last encounter made her wary and embarrassed.

He misunderstood the movement. His hand fell to his side, a flush darkened the lean cheeks. "Dammit," he muttered roughly, "don't jerk away from me like that! I'm not going to rape you!"

Sitting stiffly in the chair, Dany wanted to explain her recoil; wanted to tell him that she was tired and hurting and filled with dread by the approaching storm; wanted to tell him that she loved him, had always loved him. The only thing that emerged, however, was a tremulous question. "Do we have to stay here all night?"

He stiffened, the hectic color draining from his face and

leaving it oddly pale. "Yes," he answered evenly. "There's a tube of antiseptic in the kit; you'd better put some on that cut. I'm going to unsaddle the horse and put him in the corral."

Dany stared after him, hot tears dammed up in the back of her throat. With a tired sigh she pulled the first-aid box toward her and opened it. The tube of antiseptic lay on top of packages of gauze and Band-Aids. As she picked up the tube she noticed an elastic bandage beside it, but she felt too tired to wrap it around her ankle.

By the time Bay returned, she had smeared some of the cream on her cut. She watched him drop his saddle onto the floor and then turn a measuring eye toward the wood piled in the corner. Apparently deciding that it would last them the night, he closed the door and removed his slicker, hanging it on a peg by the door. He was still pale, his jawline taut and unyielding, and Dany felt the tension in the room increase, just as it was building outside the small cabin as the approaching storm prepared to vent its fury.

Bay bent to unroll his sleeping bag, disclosing a blanket folded within it. Without looking at her, he said, "There's a Thermos of coffee and some sandwiches in the saddlebags."

The coldness of his voice chilled her. Shivering, she rose, intending to reach across the table for the saddlebags. An unwary step sent pain crashing through her as her weight came down on the injured ankle, and she crumpled against the table, a ragged moan escaping her.

Immediately strong arms were lowering her to the chair. "You little fool!" Bay muttered angrily. "Why didn't you say something?" He knelt in front of her, the long, sensitive fingers gently examining her swollen ankle. Carefully he slipped her shoe off without commenting on its dampness, and when she bit back a cry of pain, said gruffly, "Sorry, honey, but I have to check it out."

Dany stared at his bent head, a sudden feeling of helpless love chasing away the pain of her ankle. Her eyes moved over the planes and angles of his face, watching the firelight create shifting shadows, seeing a stark beauty that she had never noticed before.

"A bad sprain," he murmured, reaching for the first-aid box. "You'll be more comfortable with it bound."

Silently Dany watched him wind the elastic bandage around her ankle, knowing her thoughts were protected by the shadows and taking advantage of it. Her hungry gaze searched out each feature, each beloved characteristic, imprinting his face on her memory.

He secured the bandage and looked up at her, unable in the dimness to read her expression. "Better?"

Huskily, her hands gripped tightly together in her lap, Dany replied, "Much better. Thank you."

He stared up at her for a long moment, slowly lowering her ankle to the floor. Then, with a harshly indrawn breath, he rose to his feet and turned to dig the Thermos from the saddlebags, his face tight. Removing the cup from the bottle, he unscrewed the lid and poured out some coffee. "Here," he said abruptly, thrusting the cup into her hands. "Drink this. You're shivering."

Dany raised the cup to her lips, grateful for the warmth even though her shivers had been caused by the touch of his hands rather than the cold. He went over to pick up the blanket, returning to stand behind her as he dropped it around her shoulders. His hands lingered for a moment, but were suddenly jerked away as she stiffened. A crash of thunder had shattered the quiet of the cabin, but he hadn't noticed that; he had only noticed her apparent rejection.

He stepped over to the fireplace, fumbling in his shirt pocket for a cigarette and lighting it with shaking hands. Expelling the smoke harshly, he said in a low voice, "I don't blame you for hating me. God knows, I brought it on myself. I thought all women were alike—grasping and deceitful—and by the time I realized you were different, it was too late. I had driven you away from me." Her face was turned away from him, but he saw a shudder pass through her slender body and burst out painfully, "God, don't shake like that! I can't stand it!"

Dany heard the words, but only perceived them on the most shallow level of her conscious mind. Everything else was completely caught up in the wild, familiar panic holding her in its cruel grip. She pushed the cup away from her blindly, staring toward the window, shaking with helpless terror, fighting to choke down the scream rising in her throat. And then the storm was directly overhead. A brilliant flash of lightning, accompanied by a savage crack of thunder, tore the violent scream from her throat, from the deepest part of her being.

The scream jerked Bay around, his face whitening. He pitched his cigarette into the fire, moving swiftly in front of her and bending to grasp her shoulders. "Dany!" He saw the stark, animal terror in her eyes and, for a moment, agony sliced through him. Then he saw that her eyes were fixed, not on his face, but on the grimy window, lighted now with the storm's raging fury.

Groaning softly, he swept her into his arms, blanket and all, sitting down on the chair and holding her rigid, trembling body in a protective embrace. "It's all right," he whispered gently, stroking the tumbled copper-gold hair. "It's all right; there's nothing to be afraid of." Obeying instincts as old as time itself, he soothed her with his hands and his voice.

His comfort brought sanity back into Dany's mind, the rigidity flowing from her limbs as she turned her face against the strong column of his neck with a dry sob. "I'm

178

sorry," she whispered raggedly. "I'm sorry, but I can't help it!"

"Don't be sorry," he told her softly. "We're all afraid of something."

"Not you." She shivered violently as another deafening clap of thunder shook the tiny cabin. "Never you."

"Even me," he whispered huskily on an odd thread of pain, turning her face up and kissing her. He meant it to be a soothing kiss, thinking of her, at that moment, as a frightened child. But the creature in his arms was no child.

Her senses heightened by the storm, her love for this man quivering in every nerve of her body, Dany responded instantly with all the passion he had taught her. Her shaking lips parted beneath his; her arms slipped up around his neck; her body trembled with a totally different feeling.

The instant, total response wrenched a groan from Bay, and his kiss deepened urgently. Passion flared between them with the violence of the storm outside, their hunger for each other sweeping all before it in a raging tide. For countless moments the fiery kiss went on, their bodies straining toward one another as though they would destroy the barriers of flesh and clothing to become one being.

Dany was not aware of being lifted and carried to the sleeping bag, or of being lowered onto its quilted softness. She felt no pain when her injured ankle touched the floor. The storm was a forgotten thing; only the man holding her so tightly in his arms had substance, had reality.

Then, quite suddenly, Bay tore his mouth from hers with an obvious effort. "Dammit, I can't. . . ." He buried his face against her neck, his body shuddering as he fought to regain control over his passion. "I can't take advantage of you, Dany," he groaned hoarsely. "You're scared, and you're hurting—and I can't take advantage of that."

179

"You won't be taking advantage, Bay," she whispered achingly. "Make love to me!" Her fingers moved soothingly over the knotted tension of his neck. "I want you to."

Another shudder racked his body, the shaking need in her voice almost more than he could bear. "God, don't you think I want to?" he demanded thickly. "I need you, Dany—more than anything on this earth—but I don't want you to hate me any more than you already do."

Abandoning her last shred of pride, Dany cried, "No, you're wrong! I don't hate you, Bay, I—"

"You don't hate me now!" he rasped. "I'm not a boy, Dany; I know I can make you want me. But you'd hate me afterward. I want more than one night of passion from you."

Suddenly uncertain, she whispered, "You said—once you said that you'd wait . . . until I was helpless—stripped bare of everything—and then you'd take me. . . ."

With a muffled curse he dragged himself away from her and sat up, staring into the fire with the oddly opaque eyes of a blind man. "I was out of my mind that night," he said roughly. "You had run from the beach to get away from me, and then when I followed you here, those beautiful eyes of yours looked right through me. I had to watch you smiling at Tremaine all evening, and I wanted to kill him. Then in your room you said that you hated me, and when you hit me, something just seemed to snap. You had me in such a state that I was making cruel threats and hurting you."

"You—it didn't seem to bother you when I said I hated you," Dany said hesitantly.

"I didn't believe you!" He laughed with harsh self-contempt. "Like the arrogant swine I was, I didn't believe you. But then when I saw what I'd done to you, I knew it was true. I saw the hate in your eyes, and it was like a knife twisting in my guts. I knew then what a fool I'd been—but by then it was too late."

Dany felt a sudden, incredulous joy building within her. Was it possible? Had Bud been right after all? Before she could ask the question trembling on her lips, Bay went on.

"I tried to stay away from you after that. God, it wasn't easy. Every time you walked into the room, my heart stopped beating; I couldn't think straight! I broke out in a cold sweat whenever you came near me. Those damn parties were murder—and the nights were pure hell!"

"Marissa?" she whispered questioningly.

He laughed mirthlessly. "I wanted you to think I didn't give a damn! I told myself it was just physical desire, that I'd get over you, but I knew it wasn't true. I was fighting like hell to keep from admitting how I really felt, and it was breaking me apart inside." His voice was a painful rasp; his face gray as he stared into the fire blindly. "I wanted you every minute of every day—and not just to make love to you, although God knows I wanted that. But what I really wanted was the right to call you *mine*. I wanted to have you at my side, and to know that only I had the right to hold you and touch you. The thought of some other man winning you nearly drove me out of my mind."

"What am I, a door prize?" Dany asked, half laughing, half serious.

He closed his eyes for an anguished moment. "You are the pot of gold at the end of the rainbow," he said deeply. "An oasis in the desert. The peace after the storm. The first flower of spring." He opened his eyes, a sigh seeming to come from deep inside him. "I wish I were a poet; I could tell you then. But I'm not, Dany. I'm a man. Just a mortal man who found to his surprise that he was no different from any other. That he could ache inside be-

181

cause of something he didn't even believe existed. That he could be torn and bleeding where no one could see."

Dany stared up at him and felt her heart move painfully within her breast. The grinding emotion in his voice was something that she had never heard before, something she never would have believed him capable of. "I love you, Bay."

He went very still, every muscle in his body knotting with tension. "Don't say it unless you mean it," he said hoarsely. "Don't say it just to torture me. I may deserve it, but don't . . . please. I don't think I could stand it."

"Bay, look at me," she pleaded softly.

Slowly, as if the move were agony for him, he turned his head, his tormented gaze meeting the shimmering darkness of her emerald eyes.

"I love you," she whispered intensely, "with everything inside of me!" The mask was gone, a tender smile curving her lips; naked, unashamed love glowed in her eyes.

With a sudden shuddering groan he came down beside her on the soft sleeping bag and gathered her into his arms, his mouth searching blindly for hers. The kiss they exchanged then was unlike any other—a tender, joyous declaration of love between them, with nothing hidden.

At last he buried his face in her neck, his body trembling in her arms. "Tell me you're mine, Dany," he whispered, his voice shaking, pleading; there was none of the cruel certainty she hated. "Tell me that Carrington and Tremaine don't matter to you."

"They don't," she answered tremulously, her eyes shining with happy tears. "Only you, Bay. No one else matters."

He lifted his head and gazed down at her with the eyes of a man who has just discovered a portion of Heaven in his hands. "God, I've needed you for so long," he said

182

unsteadily. "I think I fell in love with you the first time I saw that magazine cover you did last year."

Dany looked startled. "You mean . . . before we met?"

"Before we met," he admitted thickly. "I didn't realize it then, but I couldn't get your face out of my mind. And then, when I was working on the script for your book—not that I knew it *was* your book—I knew that I wanted you for Serena. I was furious when you refused the offer, and even more angry when I heard the rumors about you and Carrington."

A shadow crossed her eyes. "You believed them."

"No," he said quickly, framing her face with trembling hands. "I knew you weren't his mistress; I knew that the first time you looked up at me with those innocent eyes."

"Then why?" she whispered pleadingly. "Why were you so cruel about those rumors?"

"Jealousy, darling. I knew you weren't Carrington's mistress, but he was important to you, and it drove me crazy to think of another man in your life. I was so damn confused I didn't know what was wrong with me. I'd never in my life let a woman get under my skin, and then you came along and suddenly I couldn't think straight. That night at the beach, I wanted you so badly . . . and then Carrington called and the jealousy started eating at me."

Dany gently caressed his lean cheek, her senses flaring when he turned his head to softly kiss her hand. "Jason called to ask about the outline for my next book. That's what wasn't finished, why I needed more time."

He sighed heavily. "Last night, after I left you, I wondered if maybe that had been it."

"Last night," she murmured, staring up at him. "It explained so much when you told me about your mother. I knew you didn't trust women."

"I never learned to. I was blind where my mother was

183

concerned. I see that now, but at the time I only felt betrayed. My father loved her so much, and she destroyed him. I vowed right then that I'd never make myself vulnerable to a woman the way that he had. I never had any trouble keeping that promise until I met you."

His eyes had gone opaque again, his face strained. "I fought like a demon to keep from admitting how I felt about you," he said harshly. "I came here and had to watch Tremaine looking at you in those damn sexy gowns —it was hell! God, I was mooning over you like a lovesick boy and didn't realize it until yesterday morning in the garden."

Dany smoothed the lines of pain from his face with tender fingers. "You were so gentle."

The opaque look faded; he gazed down at her with darkly passionate eyes. "You looked up at me so sweetly," he murmured. "I knew then that the torment I was feeling wasn't caused by simple physical desire. I was shaking, I needed you so badly."

Dany remembered the trembling gentleness of his caresses, and knew that it was true. But then Jason had come. . . . "You were so angry and bitter when you left."

"I was bleeding," he said flatly. "I'd just admitted to myself that I couldn't live without you—and then I suddenly realized that I had driven you away from me with my stupid accusations, my brutal treatment of you. Hearing Carrington's voice made it all worse."

"That night when we were all in the great room, and everyone was so upset about my book—you were still angry."

"Carrington was with you," Bay said simply.

"And—and later?" Shyness stole into Dany's eyes. "I thought, after you left, that I had made you think I was— was cheap. After what I said, what I did—"

"When you offered to give yourself to me?" His eyes

184

flared suddenly. "God, you'll never know how hard it was for me to leave you! Forgive me, darling, I don't mean to sound crass, but I knew damn well your body was mine for the taking."

"Oh!" She laughed suddenly. "Crass? More like conceit!"

His indigo eyes glimmered with amusement. "Was I wrong?" he asked teasingly.

"No . . . damn you," she muttered, her face hot.

He pressed a brief kiss on her flushed cheek, his face tender. "That was the whole problem," he told her wryly. "I didn't think you loved me, but every time we came near each other, the physical attraction between us was so strong that nothing else seemed to matter. I wanted your heart as well as your body, and it tortured me to know that I could have one but not the other."

"If you had looked at me last night," she said softly, "you would have realized that I loved you. I couldn't hide it any longer." She allowed one finger to trace a tiny circle around the pulse beating rapidly at the base of his neck. "Bay? When I was so frightened of the storm, you said that even you were afraid of something. What is it?"

He was staring down at her, breathing roughly. "A life without you," he answered thickly. "Oh, God, Dany, I love you so much." He covered her face with feverish kisses, his lips warm and shaking. "Marry me, sweetheart . . . please."

Her eyes glowing with happiness, Dany whispered teasingly, "What would you do if I said no?"

He raised his head to stare down at her. "I'd die," he said quietly, simply.

Dany's breath caught in her throat at the stark pronouncement. Her voice filled with shaking intensity, she said, "Yes. I'll marry you—whenever you want me to."

The tension drained from his body, he rested his forehead against hers with a shuddering sigh. "Tomorrow," he whispered, his breath warm on her face. "We'll fly to Vegas. I don't think I could stand to wait any longer."

Dany ran her hands lovingly over the strong muscles of his back and shoulders, feeling them tighten beneath her touch. "Tomorrow," she murmured in agreement, her eyes gazing softly into his. "But I don't want to wait."

He caught his breath, eyes darkening with hungry eagerness. "God, you know how much I want you," he groaned hoarsely. "But I want our life together to be perfect. Darling, I don't want you to have anything to regret."

"I won't regret a thing," she whispered huskily, her fingers slowly unfastening his shirt. "I love you, Bay; I want to belong to you."

Bay stared down at her for a long moment, drinking in the love and desire he saw in her eyes. Then, with an odd sound deep in his chest, he lowered his lips to hers.

The storm raged impotently for a time, and then gradually faded away into the distance, but the two mortals within the tiny cabin never noticed.

LOOK FOR NEXT MONTH'S
CANDLELIGHT ECSTASY ROMANCES™: